MW01484200

# Jonathan Spradlin

# American Creamy

## Part 1

Lupe,

I've been a guest at your jail
on occasion on account of my
struggles with opiates. I am well
now, but I'd like you to read this
because much of it is set in the
West Tower. We share a few friends,
especially in the person of Wanda, but
and also close to Steve Springer →

*Please give me some feedback. I'd love to meet with you and discuss this book and my experiences in 2010 and 2011.*

*J. S.*

AMERICAN CREAMY (PART 1). Copyright © 2015 by Jonathan Spradlin. All rights reserved. Printed in the United States of America. No part of this publication may be reproduced, distributed, or transmitted in any form or by any means, or stored in a database or retrieval system, without the prior written permission from the author. For information about permission to reproduce sections from this book, email to Permissions, J Spradlin, at jonathanspradlin@jonathanspradlin.com

FIRST EDITION

Cover artwork, title page, map page, and graphic illustration by Joshua Davies.

Interior text design by Madeline Reiss and Kevin Klix.

Exterior Photo © 2015 by Mike Lyon.

Edited by Madeline Reiss.

Library of Congress Cataloguing-in-Publication Date is available upon request.

ISBN: 978-0-692-52478-7

1

*For my Family.*

# Jonathan Spradlin

---

# American Creamy

---

## Part 1

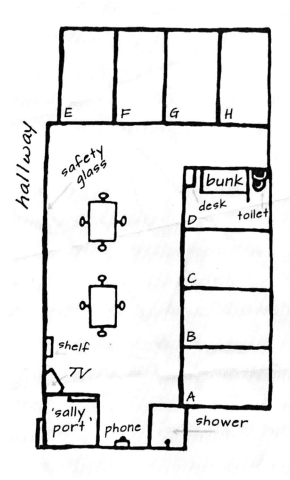

West Tower 7P1

## Part I: The Preacher Man

*None who go to her return, nor do they regain the paths of life—*
*So you may walk in the way of Goodness and keep to the paths of*
*righteousness. For the upright will dwell in the land, and the*
*blameless will remain in it; But the wicked will be cut off from the*
*earth, and the unfaithful will be uprooted from it.*
                                                              *—Proverbs 2*

*First I had faith, then I had none, and then I became the*
*bewildered one.*
                                                              *—Anonymous*

# 1.

Sitting here in this damn single cell in the West Tower at the Lew—fuck this place. Sometimes when I feel like it I just piss on the floor. What difference does it make? Guards don't give a damn. Been thinking about rubbing shit all over the walls past couple of days. That crazy? Fuck, probably it is. I'm so far beyond giving a damn right now. I rub my fingers through my curly black and silver beard, pulling on it a little. These jailhouse psych doctors don't know a damn thing about being crazy. There is no such thing as being crazy, anyway. My damn head. The man in the cell next to mine hasn't showered in weeks. This is what real people smell like. Before Dial soap and Old Spice, Chanel No. 5, or running water. When she poured the pound of fragrant oil over Jesus' perfect head, what was the perfect smell? This sick stench reeks and seeps through the cracks of my cell door, mingling with the scent of piss and orange peels.

I don't know how to tell this story, but I have to, don't I? It's not like I have a choice.

## 2.

They've been calling me Preacher Man for years, ever since my first trip down south back in '87. Nowadays, you hear the inmates yammering on about "Gladiator Farms" and "Rock n' Roll Units." Yeah, they're still around. Telford, Beto, Coffield, there's a few. Back when I started getting locked up it was all "Rock n' Roll", all violent, all killing, all fucking, all fear; all hell.

The first time I got locked up was for getting caught with a pound of dirt weed that wasn't even mine. I didn't have a job, and my Uncle Ray-Ray would pay me forty dollars to take this or that across to Cookie's house. It went off smoothly every time before. This time I'm walking down Toronto Street, about six in the afternoon, when before I knew what was happening I'm down on the ground, shots ringing out all around me.

I crawled underneath a dirty car and watched a man get shot in the face not fifty feet from me. I grew up in the hood, but I'd never seen anything like that. I guess I just froze up. I got so damn scared because I thought the dude who shot and killed that man somehow knew I'd seen him do it. No thoughts in my head but pure fear.

The next thing I know, the cops are pulling me out from under that old, broken-down Plymouth where I'd hidden for I don't know how long, along with the pound of weed I'd forgotten about. Everything was a blur. I wound up downtown at the Government Center under charges of first-degree murder. They threw me into the worst dungeon available to Dallas County at the time. This big, corn fed, white boy jailer gave me a cup and a spoon, opened up an old-ass metal door, said, "good luck, buddy," and pushed me in.

My uncles had told me about this place, so I immediately started looking for somebody I knew—hoping that there was a cat from my hood in there. I'm looking— nobody, nothing. Everybody's quiet, so I start looking for an empty cell. I hear a deep voice call out behind me, "Hey boy—hey!" Turning around, I see a monster of a man sitting at one of the steel tables, playing bones with some other fool.

"This is mah tank, boy. You fights?"
I grew up in West Dallas, so I've been fighting since I could walk. But I was 5'10", 150, and 18 years old. For the second time in twenty-four hours, I was scared out of my head. I could barely force myself to speak.

"Naw man, I don't fight."

"You don't fights? C.Q. Say, get that fool up says he's sick, ova' in L Cell."

The Tank Boss was easily 300 pounds of solid muscle. I'm watching as C.Q. grabbed some skinny fool out of a cell, guy looked like he was dying. I'd seen people in the hood coming off of heroin before, and that's what he looked like— right at death's door. I noticed he had a busted lip and swollen jaw.

"C'mon, man…," I said.

"We fights in here, boy," said the Tank Boss.

4

Apparently, the sick fool already knew the drill. He put his fists up while the other cats in the tank gathered around us. It wasn't like a fight in the hood, though. The guys watching were quiet. Silent, man. I could hear the thudding footsteps of the watchers as they gathered in. It was quiet like you leave the T.V. on at night—no sound, just for the light. For the first time in my life, I got a whiff of jail smell. The smell was cheap, stale tobacco smoke mixed with rotten food and dead skin. In those days you could smoke cigarettes.

I think my life changed when I registered that smell. No...I know it did. The boy who hid under the car was gone in an instant. Like a snap, the violence hit me. I took two steps and threw a right to the junkie's chin, and he just crumpled. Lights out. He hit the floor and started puking.

"A'ight fool," the Tank Boss pointed to another youngster. Kid was about my size. No other words, he just pointed. The kid stepped up, but I could tell by his stance that he didn't have any real skills. I think he got in one weak lick before I knocked him out cold. On the way down, he hit his head on the corner of a steel table. The blood just seeped out. I got a flash of the man shot in the head before my eyes. The two even looked a lot alike. They could have been brothers.

I was breathing hard, and I was tired. Surely, I thought, if this was some initiation, it was over now. I'm part of the club, now.

"Say!"

The Tank Boss was behind me, so I turned to face him.

"You's a lyin' muthafucka! You bouts ta get fucked-up naw! C.Q."

C.Q. was 230 solid. Or anyway, he was a hell of a lot bigger than me, and ugly as sin. Everybody in the tank was on their feet now, surrounding us in a ring. You could smell the adrenaline. They all had their shirts off, shoulder to shoulder. I looked around for a guard or some other savior, but there was no one. No way out.

C.Q. stepped at me swinging, and I tried a desperate move. I went down to a knee and punched him as hard as I could straight in the balls. He went down squealing like a stuck pig. I had a brief feeling of jubilant triumph before the fear took over again. Hands went under my arms and I was kicking and screaming, using fingernails and teeth on any piece of exposed flesh I could find.

The silence broke as twenty men's voices yelled in a frenzy. The Tank Boss and two others threw me into one of the cells. I remember looking over at the bunk into the eyes of a man lying there. Not every inmate was in the ring after all. He looked at me with terror in his eyes, and then covered his head with his blanket.

I stood up and faced the Tank Boss. He was laughing at me. I knew I had no chance, but I tried a punch anyway. My fist just bounced off his face, he didn't even bother blocking it. He laughed again and threw me down to the concrete. I was so far beyond fear that I didn't feel anything at all. Since then I've learned about the fight or flight response, and I suppose I was in the middle of that. I don't know. The Tank Boss pulled out his stinking member and said, "Nah you gonna suck my dick."

I screamed. I yelled, "Fuck you, bitch!" I kicked out as hard as I could, directly at the man's penis. As my foot struck flesh, I remember thinking *Help me God* before all went black stars.

**I** woke up in a hospital bed. Both of my arms were in casts; I couldn't see out of one of my eyes. I couldn't move my jaw. A nurse came into the stale, dingy room.

"Thank goodness," she said. "Thank goodness."

I looked over and noticed that my left foot was cuffed to the bed, and it all came flooding back—memories like physical experiences. No analysis—just images, sounds, smells—pain. I passed back into a dark dream.

## 4.

I was in a coma for three weeks. I still have a plate and a scar on the left side of my skull where it was cracked and punctured. In all, I had fourteen broken bones from the brawl, and my jaw had to be wired back together where it was split at the chin. I was a wreck. But when the police came to visit me, they were unapologetic:

"Mr. Thomas, the murder charge against you has been dropped. The culprit in that crime has been identified. But, in regards to the marijuana found in your possession of at the time of your arrest, you are charged with a felony in the second degree."

I was hospitalized four months. All that time I was in and out of surgery, lost in a haze of pain and drugs. I have no memory of it, but during that time I somehow pled guilty to the possession charge and was given three years TDC time. Commonplace railroad job.

As I was getting close to being healthy enough for release from Parkland Hospital, a man from the parole board visited me. I remember that he was corpulent, and he stank of old cigars. It reminded me of that first whiff of jail scent. He wore a plaid coat, and his neck was so fat his shirt collar wouldn't button. While looking at the collar, I noticed a little brown stain just below where his nasty, fat flesh bulged over.

He was riveting as he stood there looking down at me, holding his scuffed, reddish, leather briefcase. Time seemed to slow down under his beady gaze. Pieces of him separated themselves for me and became distinct entities. His unkempt, longish, dirty-brown hair. His bristly mustache, half-covering pasty, slobbering fat lips. Coke bottle glasses that framed his eyes of startlingly pale green. Once I penetrated the glasses and really gazed into his eyes, I couldn't look away. The weakness from my injuries felt logarithmically weaker. I felt like a child. Not afraid really, just very small; tiny before this huge manifestation.

It was the sound of his breathing—the heavy, labored breath of the morbidly obese—that awoke me from my fixation. He took a sharp breath, thumped over to the chair next to my bed, and eased his bulk into it with a great sigh.

A gift is a curse when you're at your neighbor's house, and I don't know whether I've ever been home or not, but the moment that fat man sat down I thought, *I am not the same. Something's different. I am not the same.* I've called it *the cream* ever since, if I call it anything at all. What I mean by that is when you smell shit, you usually don't think about having a nose; when you see a flower in blossom, you may think *red rose,* but you don't think about your eyes. Not unless you are a poet or a philosopher, and God help you if you've been cursed with that problem. No, instead you just see, smell, feel, think— it's part of what you are, like being 6'2" or having big feet or a little dick. You're different and you know it, but you adapt and move on. Stick and move.

Today, after I shit, I caught myself looking at a little piece of it floating there in the stainless steel toilet/sink combo provided for me here in my cell at the West Tower of the Lew. I rolled up one of the sheets of white paper that I am writing this story on into a tight little tube, and I held it there a long time—a few minutes, half an hour maybe—I don't know. I contemplated moving the little log around with it. I kept shaking my head and turning away from the toilet/sink. It didn't really stink, not any more than the rest of this place, but I kept getting stuck. I wasn't staring at the shit, I was thinking about moving it— looking at the little tube of paper with pieces of words turning in a spiral.

Finally, I noticed another inmate out in the dayroom looking into my cell at me, and I reached up and pushed the flush button. *Whoooosh!* the loud suction of water reverberated throughout my cell.

"Can I help you?" I said to the white boy looking at me. He hurriedly turned his face back up to the TV. "Stay out my cell, motherfucka!"

Number one rule when you are locked up with animals — Don't look in the cage. Don't look in their eyes.


What shocked me most about the fat man who came to see me in the hospital was what came out of his mouth.

"Mr. Thomas? Ezekiel Thomas?"

It took me a moment to respond because of his accent. Looking back, I'm pretty sure it was British. I recognized it from watching Monty Python.

"Yeah? Who are you?'"

My jaw was no longer wired shut, but I was unused to speaking. My uncles would come visit me once a week on Sundays if they weren't too busy, but we didn't really speak much. Half the time Ray-Ray was trying to figure out how to steal the morphine, anyway.

"My name is Mr. Lourdes, and I work for the Texas Department of Pardons and Paroles. I'm here to inform you, Mr. Thomas, that the parole board has voted to grant you parole *in absentia* from the custody of the Texas Department of Corrections once you are cleared for release from Parkland Hospital…have you a place of residence, sir? Excuse me." *Cough, Cough!*

The fat British man's face turned a shade of purple-red that was like a drying rose petal pressed into a diary. He coughed and spat, and a globby speck of blood and phlegm landed on my left hand. He then bent and vomited roughly into the trashcan to the right of his chair. He took another moment to gather himself, wiping his mustache and chin with a filthy handkerchief held by stubby, greasy fingers.

"You must forgive me, Mr. Thomas. I've been ill, you understand."

I asked him if he'd like me to press the red button for the nurse.

"No. Thank you, young man, but I'm quite all right."

I reached for a tissue and slowly wiped the man's discharge from my hand, trying not to draw his attention to the fact that he had coughed upon me so disgustingly. Whatever the outcome of the interview, I wanted this creature out of my presence without further drama. Mr. Lourdes pushed his fat body out of the chair with a great exertion of force, placed his briefcase upon the swivel-tray attached to my bed where the orderlies would normally place my meals. He opened it and withdrew some documents, along with a large, expensive-looking, black and gold pen. Funny how I remember the pen so well—how it seemed to fit the size of a man like Lourdes. I think it must have been a gift from a considerate loved-one. Perhaps a sister or daughter.

"Sign here, here, and here, along with the date and it is ah—January the eighteenth. You must report to the parole office within twenty-four hours of your release from Parkland. You are a free man. I've already dismissed your guard."

Lourdes was smiling at me, but it looked like the smile

of a fat skull. He made a sound deep in his throat as he reached into his jacket pocket and removed a small key. Still smiling, he placed the key into the lock of my leg cuff. As he leaned down, I saw a blood vessel burst in the white of his right eye. So violent was the burst that a little droplet of blood, like a tear, fell from his eye onto the white of my sheet. Leaving the key in the lock, Lourdes put his hands up to his throat in the universal choking/ahogo stance while blood continued to drip steadily from his eye.

I was about to shout and push the nurse-call button when the man fell, his temple connecting directly with the sharp corner of the chest of three drawers next to my bed.

"Christ," I said.

I could only stare in silence as thick blood gushed from the man's head. His bloodshot eye stared up at me, and his corpulent lips were still twisted into the ghost of a smile. Lourdes was dead. Lourdes was a Parole Officer. Lourdes's head was cracked open like a snake-bitten bluebird egg in an ill-founded bird's nest. I was a young black man in Texas, chained to a bed in 1983. I was a young black man smart enough to know that the cops weren't about to believe me when I told them that the fat man slipped and fell. I could hear it in my head, "I swear Officer! His eye went bloodshot and he went down, right after he put the key in the lock!" Hell no.

With the buzz of the impending electric chair humming in my ears, I gingerly reached down to my leg cuff and turned the key in the lock.

*Click.*

I was free.

I was still hurting all over, but my legs hadn't been injured that badly. I could walk. I could even run. Part of my rehab had been walking up and down the halls of the wing with a nurse and a guard. I knew where the stairs were. I slipped off the bed, avoiding Lourdes's blood, and opened the door into the hall, peeking to make sure the guard was gone, as the fat man had told me. The hall was empty aside from a nurse dressed in white, all the nurses wore white back then, stepping quietly with her back to me. The sounds I'd grown accustomed to—doctor's being called here or there with various codes over the loudspeaker—washed over me.

It struck me that I had changed from the boy I once was, growing up in the West Dallas 'hood. I knew I should have been shaking like hell spawn in Alaska right then, but I wasn't; my heart rate wasn't even up. Oh, I've been plenty scared since then, believe that. But I wasn't scared in that hospital.

I needed to get a coat or a jacket to cover myself up. All I had on was that damn hospital gown, split in the back. First though, I had to get off the floor where all the nurses and doctors and orderlies knew my face. I walked, calm and easy, to the back stairs nearest my room, and went down from the fourth to the second floor. They'd walked me down there before, and I had seen into a few of the rooms. It looked like some sort of cancer ward with half the patients on breathing machines. I glanced into the first room and slipped inside. The old man residing there was asleep with drool sliding out of his half-open mouth into a puddle on his from-home pillow case.

I walked over to his closet, opened the door, and *Bingo* my luck was holding so far. Old, rich, white son-of-a-bitch had a goddam all-white suit, pressed and laundered, hanging there waiting for him. No shit man, I had to look back at the geezer to make sure he wasn't Colonel F. Sanders. He favored him in a way, with his skinny ass. Right about then I would have kissed that white man's ass though, and there was something else— something about that suit—how can I describe it so that it can be understood?

It's another idea like the sense of *the cream*. When the fat man came into my room I didn't know what the hell was wrong with me. But as I opened the closet door in the old, white

14

man's room, the white suit shone out at me, it glowed. It was like a jigsaw piece, hanging there. I don't know if I knew the word back then, but I know now what I felt—affinity.

I dressed in the suit, which fit me perfectly—even the shoes. I didn't go delving through the chest looking for underwear, and instead decided to free ball it, which was fitting. I walked out the front doors of Parkland hospital free as a bird; dick aloof in the January wind.

6.

I caught myself staring at the toilet again. There wasn't any shit or piss in it this time, just clear, cold water. It was real quiet, middle of the night. I could see the water perfectly though, because here in the West Tower, the lights never go off. Don't ever again in your life complain about the harsh fluorescent lighting in your office, asshole, don't you do it. Just don't. I'm staring at the water and I see these little waves like vibrations on the surface. I lower my head into the bowl, just above the water, and I close my eyes. Like whispers, I hear the echoing sound of voices. Female voices. I strain to hear what they are saying, but the words are indistinct. The only thing I can make out is the same woman, a black girl by the sound of her voice, raising it to say, "Hell Naw!" and later, "Best friend..." like she was addressing someone.

A little teardrop drips from my eye and plops into the toilet water as a memory hits me like slow lightning—

"You my best friend, E?"

Lexi's sweet, soft, seductive voice pulls at me and opens

some young place of longing from years and years ago. It was 1986, in the middle of August. Lexi's small, pale, white hand caressed my muscular black arm while we lay in bed at the Tampico motel over on East Grand by White Rock Lake. The old, noisy A/C unit by the window coughed and blew and compressed like a heavy smoker trying to run a mile. The cool air coming out of the machine shifted the curtains of the large window, periodically letting in blinding bars of a burning sunlight, throwing everything it struck into stark relief.

"Ezekiel? Are you my best friend?" Lexi asked me again.

I just looked at her. It didn't matter whether I answered or not, not to her anyway. She rubbed her perfectly shaped legs against mine and said, "Yeah you are, yeah you are."

She closed her eyes and smiled in a moment of perfect contentment, snuggling her cheek against my shoulder. My room was number 214, upstairs on the corner. It was close to the stairs so I could hear people coming up. As I thought of it, I heard one set of footsteps bounding up in a hurry. I grabbed my little, .38 revolver from under the pillow and strode to the door, pushing Lexi aside. A shadow crossed the curtains and stopped. There was a faint knock.

"Yeah?" I said.

"It's Darryl," a voice answered.

"Cover up," I told Lexi.

I slapped open the chain lock and ushered the man inside.

"Muthafucka, I told you not to come over here unless you called first."

"C'mon man."

"C'mon nothin', white boy," I said. "I ought to break yo' shit."

I lifted the gun up over my shoulder like I was about to bust his skull with it. He cringed convincingly enough for me to lower the weapon, walk around the bed to where my Levis were, and pull them on—slipping the .38 through the waistband. I glanced over at Lexi who was sitting cross-legged on the bed with the cheap, dingy sheet wrapped around her breasts. She held my gaze. It took me a moment to realize, through my haze of anger, that she had *the cream*. That feeling washed through me—a memory of Tank Boss standing over me with his monstrous grin painted itself atop my vision in little spots and flashes, then a dreadlocked man bleeding, sitting at a campfire, before my vision faded back to just Lexi on the bed.

She consumed me. But it wasn't lust, or at least not lust alone. I watched as she reached over to the bedside table and removed a long, skinny cigarette from her pack of Virginia Slim menthols with a pale, freckled, sensual arm. Her shoulder length, straightened, deep-auburn hair half-covered her elfin face as she angled it down to lightly touch the flame of her lighter to the little tip of her cig. I looked up into the mirror that was hung on the ceiling above my bed, and my eyes were drawn to the bright, etiolate pink of her left nipple peeking out from behind the sheet. She pulled on her cigarette and her eyes glanced at me and then into the mirror to meet mine. Déjà vu hit me like a mild drug. *The cream* eased from her eyes through the mirror and into mine.

"The fuck do you want, Darryl?" I spat, without taking my eyes from the mirror. I could see him in it, too. He was staring at Lexi and trying to hide it. "You come here to steal my girl from me?"

His eyes snapped away from her as she giggled, and he looked back over at me with renewed fear. I could imagine his thoughts because he was shaking. Lexi's cigarette was giving me that jail whiff. I glanced down and saw the bulge in Darryl's little shorts, the kind you'd see those fools wearing back then. Orange and peach. Or light blue with a thin white stripe.

"The fuck you want before I get in your shit for real."

Darryl pulled a black wallet out of his back pocket and

slipped out a hundred dollar bill.

"First I need some shit man, some scag, and a couple 'ludes. You're fucking scaring the shit out of me."

"Sit down," I said.

I took the bill and walked back to the bathroom. I pulled some heroin and Quaaludes out of the stash spot. I put the dope in my pocket and almost walked out when I saw the little Daisy BB gun I'd picked up the day before at Ace Hardware when I was buying tools to fix up my stash. I pumped it up with a laugh, jumped out from the bathroom, stepped over to Darryl and shot him straight in his crotch that was still bulging.

He shouted, "Ak!"

I laughed, and Lexi started laughing too, so I pumped the Daisy again, turned, and shot her in the big nipple she was still showing.

"You fuck!" she screamed.

"Shut up," I said, still chuckling. I couldn't stop laughing. I was hysterical. I saw a tiny drop of blood on the sheet by Lexi and I finally settled down.

"Goddamit, E!" Darryl said.

"Aw, I'm sorry man, shit– here." I threw the dope and the downers onto the table next to him. He picked up one of the Quaaludes and downed it without water. I shook my head. A motherfucker ever shot me in the dick with a BB gun, I'd be shoving it down his throat about seven seconds later.

"You don't call me first next time, and you get me caught up, I'm gonna shoot you in the dick with this .38. Now get the fuck out."

Darryl held up a hand.

"E, man, there's something else, man. You gotta hear this but I uh– man, I gotta tell you in private." He cut his eyes at Lexi. I knew there was more to the story, to Darryl's visit, when Lexi glowed with *the cream* like she had. I was just getting ready for it.

"Lexi, get dressed and go get us a bottle of wine from the quick stop."

Tears in her eyes, she stood up in the middle of the bed and let the sheet fall from her naked body. I can still remember every inch of that girl like I could see her now. That perfect, 19-year-old, innocent face was staring up at me through the cold water of this stainless toilet. She blew me a kiss and took her sweet-ass time pulling her panties up her legs, bending over a little and pointing her ass right at Darryl as she slipped them over her hips. I didn't give her the satisfaction of a single word as she lit another cigarette, grabbed her tiny, silly-ass purse, and blew smoke into my smiling face. She walked out and slammed the door shut behind her. I dropped the smile and looked hard at my visitor.

"You like that, white boy?"

"Uh…Uh…naw, man. Uh…"

"Shut the hell up. That's why you'll never have a girl like that. Oh, you may luck up on enough money one day to buy one, but you'll never *have* her, not like I do– Now spit it out. What do you want?"

"Well, ah– something happened, man. I met somebody. And he's crazy, man. He's a fucking freak show, and…"

"Wait, wait, wait.    Slow down and start from the beginning."

I had a feeling this story was going to be important for some reason, so I tried to project calmness at the man. I needed to get him to get it out before the 'lude started hitting him too hard. Darryl took a deep breath.

"Oh, okay.   My little cousin, Marcus, goes to Bishop Lynch right? With a bunch of rich fucker's kids, and anyway, Marcus has this garage apartment that his parents basically let him party in and whatever behind their house. My uncle is a criminal defense lawyer and—well anyway. I hang out there with Marcus and a couple of his buddies from Lynch. I charge them double for the shit I buy from you. Dude, last night I'm over there, and we're getting FUBAR, and I don't remember how, but we end up at this huge fucking mansion, man. I mean we are walking through the door basically puking on each other, and there's like a butler with a goddam British accent—like fucking Jeevesy or something—asking me if 'there's anything else you might need, sir' and I'm like this is fucking gnarly."

"Please get to the point, Darryl," I say. I caught myself rubbing the butt of my pistol.

"Dude. I black out for a while, for sure. Then the next thing I remember, I'm taking a breath, gasping, and I'm looking down, and there's this old fucker with his sleeves rolled up on his knees next to me, pulling a syringe out of my arm."

"The fuck?" I interrupted. "Was he a doctor, or something?"

"Yeah man, that's what I thought at first, too. Then I realize I'm rushing off the biggest shot of meth I've ever done. Still, I figured he just maybe gave it to me 'cause he thought I was ODing 'til this fucker picks up another needle full, ties off, and hits *himself* with it! Right hand to the Man, E. Check it out. This dude's seas over three, man. It's just me and him in this game room—parlor room—and he's out of his gourd, and so am I, man. I'm fucking whizzed. I'm still going."

"Hang on, Darryl." I got up and yanked the pull-tab off of a warm Budweiser, fumbled in my pocket for a couple 10mg Valium, and shoved the beer and pills at him. He swallowed the Valium with a huge swig.

"Thanks, bro," he said. "Um, ah—yeah, so we start talking and I'm laughing 'cause the cat says he knows President Reagan, and shit. And after a while I'm looking at him and I realize who in the fuck I'm tweakin' with—"

He looked at me, and I looked back into his fazed-out eyes and I raised my eyebrows. He stumbled on a word, but then lowered his voice and leaned in conspiratorially to whisper.

"It was Max Parrot, man. Max fucking Parrot."

I really was surprised.

"Parrot Oil?" I asked.

"Yes, dude! Max fucking Parrot shot me up with methamphetamines! Last night! And that's not even close to being the end of it, man. I hope…uh…well, I kind of took liberties…"

*Here it comes*, I thought. *The shoe is about to drop.* The question was whether or not it was about to drop on me.

"What'd you do, Darryl?"

"Well, I figured you'd want in, man, 'cause there's a lot of money involved…a *lot*. And when he asked me, you were the one I thought of. I mean, I was just freaked out. I knew you would know what to do."

"What did he ask you, Darryl?" I could feel my temp going up.

"He said he wants a girl…"

"A girl?" I snapped. "Darryl, Max Parrot doesn't need me for that, or you. What, he wants underage? I don't play that shit."

"No…uh, he said he wants a girl– to kill. Oh yeah, and um– I hope you don't mind but– he's downstairs right now, sitting in my car."

I sat back on my bed. I happened to glance down at the little spot of Lexi's blood.

"–with a briefcase full of cash, man. He's fucked-up and he wants to do it right now. He wants to *kill* a girl right now, E."

I took a couple of deep breaths.

"Better bring him on up," I said. *Bendable Christ.*

## 7

*For the lips of an immoral woman drip honey, and her*
*mouth is smoother than      oil; But in the end she is bitter*
*as wormwood, sharp as a two-edged sword. Her feet go*
*down to death, her steps lay hold of hell. Lest you ponder*
*her path– her ways are unstable; you do not know them.*

*-- Proverbs 5*

They call this floor of the jail where I've been housed *Behavioral*
*Observation*. This is where they put you when they are pretty
sure you are at least a little bit whacko, but they haven't been
able to prove that you're the one who's been pulling his piece
out and shooting loads all over the safety glass. I don't wonder
why they put me in here. I can see it when they look into my
eyes during the examinations—the psych doctors, I mean.
Psychiatrists are some of my favorite kinds of people, to tell the
truth. I can always tell which of them are the Freudians. And
most analysts have a Freudian soul, whether they admit it to

themselves or not. At some point during the interview, they invariably look up from their notes and gaze into my eyes. A few of them find what they are looking for; I'd see their details shift and redefine themselves in my head.

One doctor had on those round, gold-rimmed glasses and they caught the fluorescent light—shooting flashes at me in a way I had a hard time ignoring. The light shone off his bald pate as well. His thick, well-trimmed, silver beard lent him an air of sophistication that was in no way deserved. I'm sure he hid it well, had there been an outside observer, but to me, as we spoke, his growing excitement was clear. A special little fire that he'd been tending somewhere inside his twisted psyche suddenly came ablaze; his hazel eyes reached out and exacted the price from me. He took from me his release, and in return his filth entered me after the fashion that it has been with so many others.

So many…so many that in prison the inmates, and even the bosses, started calling me Preacher Man. Everyone has a nickname in this fucking place anyway, if you stick around long enough to get one. (Shit-stain was always my favorite. I've known three gentlemen by the name.) I liked Preacher Man. It fit somehow, and it served my purposes. Don't mistake me, though. This *cream*, this exchange, wasn't about any sort of healing—or not always anyway.

The psychiatrist was a perfect example. I don't know or care what his diagnosis of me was, but I knew without question that as soon as he finished his appointments for the day he would be stepping sure-footedly into the bathhouse in Uptown. A place he'd driven by in trepidation without stopping a thousand times before finally stepping inside, finding the youngest male hustler in the joint, flipping him a fifty, and going down on him like an old pro. I also knew that the bathhouse antic was only the start. His tastes would begin to run younger and younger until, eventually, he'd become a walking plague of pedophilia: a sick, pus-filled sac of pain and ugliness.

That was the price a psychiatrist took from me, the Preacher Man.

This time the psych was some foreigner, a woman. She was Indian or Pakistani, I think. You see more and more of them this past decade—foreigners working in the jails and prisons. Americans don't want its ugly reality shoved into their faces anymore. They don't want to believe that thousands of their fellow citizens are locked in cages right down the street from their precious little four-bedroom houses, where Santy leaves perfectly wrapped presents under colorfully adorned pine trees for Christmastime. The time of year when Daddy finally gives in and buys little Ginger an iPhone, mainly because Mommy really thinks it would be fine, meaning she is *so* tired of hearing little Ginger whine about it, and Daddy is hoping that if he can help get little Ginger off of Mommy's nerves, then maybe Daddy gets a chance to cram it into Mommy's poop chute on Christmas Eve, Amen!

This Indian lady psych—she didn't have the dot on her head, so she's Muslim (I guess)—she just looked at my records and assigned me here, which is fine by me, honestly. I get my own cell, and there's only eight of us on the tank. These fools are in here for different reasons. I just stay in my cell anyway. A white boy named Johnny over in D cell got placed in here on account of the straight line cuts marching down his arm. He's lucky they didn't put him on suicide watch. Fucking asshole two cells down is burnt on wet, what they used to call "sherm" back in my day. Formaldehyde. Embalming fluid mixed with PCP. Fool's over there talking to himself right now. That, or maybe he's talking to me. I've heard him say, "Preacher man" a time or two, but then again he also keeps saying, "Man, don't spray that shit in here on me! Man, I'm trippin', man, I'm trippin', hey…"

He's over there covering his vent with wet toilet paper. He'll be lucky if I don't end up strangling his burnt-up neck.

Goddamit! That was the cell Eben was in before they came and got him. Eben and his fucking story. I've got to get it out of me before I scratch my eyes out. Fuck it. Fuck it. Fuck it.

I can see the TV from my cell. This cat, maybe a little older than me, is sitting at the table by himself, and he's watching the fucking *Partridge Family*. With my cell door closed, I can't make out all the words, just that it's quick, clipped, humorous conversation punctuated by the audience laugh track going off every five seconds or so. Bonaduce with his red hair shining at me brings Lexi back to mind, with her sassy little fine ass. The *Partridge Family* brings back memories of my youth. I always hated that show, along with the Monkees, and all of those fake counter-culture fashion projects.

"C'mon, get happy! C'mon, get happy!" I remember hearing the theme song on the day my uncle Larry busted into the front door with my skinny 12-year-old ass sitting on the couch and rolling a joint out of his weed tray. Uncle Larry stopped cold and so did I, just closing up the little pinner. Looking calm, but eyes red, he closed the few steps to the couch and removed the tray from my lap carefully, so as not to spill his weed. It was one of those old Coca-Cola drink trays with the stylized trademark over a smiling white man holding a Coke bottle. I know he got it out of my Big Momma's pantry. He put his tray back under the couch before straightening and snatching the little joint out of my shaking fingers.

"Hey Ezekiel," he said.

"H–hey, Uncle Larry."

"You know, this is a pretty good little joint, nephew."

I took my first breath since he walked in. The *Partridge Family* was still on and I could hear the laugh track kicking off. He put the joint in his mouth.

"Been practicing your rolling techniques, huh?"

"N–naw, Uncle Larry–"

My world went white as his huge hand cocked back and caught me in the left side of the face. My ear started buzzing and ringing. I felt one fat tear drip from my left eye.

"Don't you lie to me! Matter of fact–!"

*Thump! Thump!* He hit me so hard in the chest that my head snapped back to pop the wall behind the couch. I thought my skull was cracked. In a daze, I looked over at the TV with Bonaduce's stupid, grinning face and the sound of another fake-ass audience laugh and applause.

"Oh you grown nah, huh nephew? You's a man nah? You even been going ta school? I knew I been missin' some of mah weed."

I knew he might hit me some more, but he wouldn't hurt me too bad. I didn't give a damn right then, anyway.

"Fuck you, Uncle Larry! Fuck you, man! Why you worried 'bout whether I go to school? You can't even talk right! If you gave a damn, you'd know I was making straight A's, old fat ass dude! Yeah, I've been smoking your shit, Negro. What now? Big Momma's the only one who gives a damn about me in this house. Look at these shoes I got to wear. Fuck you, Larry."

I can't lie and say I didn't cringe back a little right then. I was surprised that I was able to get it all out without getting popped. Larry was one of the biggest bruisers in the 'hood and he'd only been back from the pen for less than a year. He was one of those types of men that look angry all the time, no matter what the occasion. I'm sure he never in his life had sex with a woman without pulling her hair and saying, "Yeah, bitch!" at least twenty times, or so. Looking back, his women were always mean, big, and talking cash-shit morning, noon, and night. And dark. Larry liked his women black as a shadow.

27

I braced for the punches, but they never came. I chanced a look up at his face, and his lips were smiling around my little joint.

"Goddam, nephew."

He withdrew a red and white book of matches, struck one, and touched the little flame to the tip of the doobie. He took a big hit and the pungent, skunk aroma of *cannabis indica* filled my nose and tickled my brain. He passed it over to me with a thumb and forefinger, and after a moment of hesitation, I grabbed and started pulling on the thing, immediately coughing my head off. My uncle laughed like crazy.

"Let me show you how to roll a real joint, nephew. This'n ain't gonna do it."

As he sat down on the couch next to me and pulled out the tray, the credits rolled on the *Partridge Family*. Not for the first time I thought to myself, *what would the white folks watching that show think if they'd just been presented with my little scene of drama?* Shit, at least the laugh track wouldn't be fake. Larry turned off the boob tube and put on a Miles Davis record.

8.

*These six things the Lord hates, yes, seven are an abomination to him: A proud look, a lying tongue, hands that shed innocent blood. A heart that devises wicked plans, feet that are swift in running to evil. A false witness who speaks lies, and one who sows discord among brethren.*

*- Proverbs 6*

Oh God, please exist.

I've learned. I know that death and blood aren't evil, that even fear has its place. I've heard a woman's voice so sweet and stayed to listen, knowing she had a blade for me hidden in the fold of her flesh. I've heard of witches and psychics. I've heard of string theory. God, please be and cancel this. Cancel it—

I could never forget the day I met Eben. How could I? It started a lot like today. In my tank, nobody has a hot pot. A hot pot is just a plastic pitcher with a hotplate at the base built in. It plugs in to the wall. If there were a use for such a thing in the free world, I'm sure you could buy one at the dollar store for—well, a dollar. Maybe two. But here, this fancy little appliance runs you fifteen bucks off the commissary cart. That, along with your standard packs of Maruchan ramen noodles (90 cents), pinkstuff coffee sweetener (10 cents per 1 gr. packet), tiny bags of off brand chips ($1.30)—basically everything is marked up anywhere from a hundred to a thousand percent or more above what you pay at the Piggly-Wiggly.

No hot pot, no hot water. I have some instant coffee, so I just use lukewarm out of my toilet/sink. It gets you there. Coffee is called John Wayne when you do it the rough way. Hell, what's a little John Wayne coffee when your bed is a three-inch-thick plastic mat laid over a raised concrete slab? Fuck, I'm in the lap of luxury here in my one-man cell with my own private shitter and this desk at the end of my slab. A piece of steel bolted to the wall for me to write on. I feel privileged. That's what happens when you've been locked up for as long as I have. *Institutionalized* means a whole lot of different things to a whole lot of different folks. It's hard to pin down, but you know it when you see it—huh, that's how defense attorneys define reasonable doubt to a trial jury. "The law won't let us define reasonable doubt anymore, but *you'll know it when you see it.*" Just like reasonable doubt in a trial, you'll know institutionalization when you see it *if you care enough to look.* Or if and until you are forced to look.

When Eben came into 7P1 three weeks ago—well, sometime in March anyway—it was a morning exactly like every other morning here. I usually stay up all night because the night is relatively quiet. People are sleeping, or reading, or rocking back and forth on their little imaginary racecars to hell, and the TV is off. Finding silence is like striking gold in these places. Some of the worst fights I've either been in or seen have been over noise. You can't get away from these assholes. You. Can't.

Get. Away. Like right now. Like right Jesus-pickin' now, this fool in my tank figured out that if you take the water out of your toilet, and the girl in the cell above does the same, then you can talk to each other. The words are indistinct, but I can tell they are having "phone sex" via the toilet plumbing. I'm laughing and half-listening, dick getting somewhat stiff—I cannot deny, because I can hear the girl. It's the same girl I heard last night. I'm also getting the visual of the two, faces in nasty stinking bowls, mumbling and moaning, breathing in the rank smell of methane gas and urine.

That shit wasn't going on while Eben was in here. I don't think so anyway. Those were strange days. It was barely before breakfast when he arrived, four o'clock in the morning. So I was up, lost in a twisted memory, when a sound that I hear twenty times a day, the machine whir and squeal of the outer sally port door rolling open, startled me so that I jumped. Something was happening. Trepidation wormed up from my toes and feet and through my legs with the opening of the door, like the harmonic nervous effect of nails on a chalkboard.

I'm in cell A, closest to the door. I looked out and saw two of the blue-suit guards escorting a white man into the tank. When I saw him I felt my entire body go into shock. It was the shock of a fear that I hadn't known since I was a small child lying in bed, staring into the dark of an open closet. I registered his appearance, but I wouldn't be able to describe it now, had that been the only time I saw him. A little explanation: Since that night in the government center with Tank Boss, or the time in the hospital after, I periodically run across people that glow with *the cream*. When I see this, I know things about these people, past or future. It takes countless forms, but the feeling is more or less the same every time. It always seems to grow from the same root, though it's never consistent. I've had entire years when it would happen almost every day, and then other times when it would happen so seldom that I would begin to believe that *the cream* was dying in me. At its worst, I feel strung along like a puppet, all free choices just *gone*. These are the troublesome times that often land my ass back in prison, like the fiasco back in '86 with Lexi and Max Parrot, the madness of A.J. the Jamaican, or San Diego in '99. I'm getting to be older now. I thought I'd seen about all that *the cream* had to show me.

But nothing, nothing I'd ever seen or felt had prepared me for the intensity of the experience that was a body striding across the day room, carrying his mat and property bag to his cell. He passed mine and glanced in, but showed no sign that he thought it odd that I was staring at him with my mouth open. He was moving into C cell, the only one that was empty. He passed out of my view, and I could hear him throw his mat down and begin rustling through his property. The blue-suits followed and slammed his cell door shut behind him. We were still locked down for the night.

After the sally port doors squealed and clanked shut behind the guards, the silence was deafening. All I could hear was the ringing in my ears and the soft *whush* of the air blowing from my vent. Jail is never that quiet, never. There is always something to break the silence—a cough, a snore, a fart, a distant toilet flush—something. I could feel the quietness pushing against my flesh as if it was liquid, and I was submerged and lying at some dark bottom.

For what seemed like an hour, I couldn't breathe. All I could do was stare at my perfectly still phantom of a reflection in the safety glass of my cell-front. The spell wasn't broken until I heard the door roll over at two tank, and the two diabetics stepped out to go to the infirmary for their insulin shots. As they ghosted out the sally port door, with its mechanical hum, I laid back with only echoes in my head. Echoes and lost voices.

fi           fi           fi

Before Darryl could leave, I heard Lexi's light, rushing footfalls coming up the stairway.

"Open the door," I said.

Darryl jumped up and did as I asked. Lexi nearly bowled him over, laughing as she came into my room.

"Oh my God," she said, with a mock-scandalized look on her face. She sat the sack she was carrying down on the table next to Darryl.

"Darryl, I'm walking through the parking lot past your car, and I saw something moving in there. This old geezer with a huge hard-on is in there totally staring at me while he's jerking off!"

Her laugh was so musical and carefree, exulting so purely and innocently in the raw pleasure she so obviously felt from the experience of walking up on Max Parrot masturbating in Darryl's Toyota Corolla, that I felt a rush of desire for her. She was so perfect, too perfect for me. My eyes caressed her lines, and for the hundredth time I wondered at her proportions. She expressed femininity in a way that was shocking to a man. Utterly shocking, and to me, even mystical. There was something of the fey to her. Looking at one such as she, there was no mystery as to the origins of the myths of fairies and nymphs. The old stories were told about real powers, real visions; real people.

"Darryl," I said, "Go tell your cock-happy friend that I'll be down in a few minutes with the redhead he just watched go up the stairs. Tell him to go ahead and get into the back seat, she'll be getting back there with him—we'll all be leaving together. You'll be driving. You got gas in that fucking car?"

"Yeah, 'bout half a tank—"

"Alright."

"What the hell, E?" Lexi said.

"Relax, sugar…Darryl, just stay down there. Crank up the AC, we'll be down in a few."

I knew we didn't have long, so even as Darryl was shutting the door, I was pulling Lexi down onto the bed and pulling her t-shirt off. I felt her shocked pleasure as I teased with my lips and tongue the nipple I had shot with the BB gun.

"Oh, God," she breathed.

Lexi was a deviant, and female, sexual deviance comes out in many different ways than male deviance. She was a true nympho; a screamer. Intellect played utterly no part in the process. That would have to come later in her life when every man who looked at her stopped doing so with the eyes of a predator. It was Lexi's father who had made her this way—made her equate sexual pleasure with acceptance. Her price from me was her release, and in exchange I tasted her subtle madness.

I tore off her little shorts and panties, and she used her legs to pull off my Levis. Her thighs were already slick with wetness; the brief view I had of her swollen labia, so perfectly formed and inviting, drove me wild. She was screaming from the moment I entered her—digging her nails into the muscles of my shoulders; squirming in a complete loss of physical control. I didn't even try to hold myself back. I fucked her like we were animals. Pure feline. Her screams rose in pitch, and I joined in as I climaxed in that moment of transcendence that sex can sometimes bring.

Panting, I covered her sweat-filmed face with kisses before rolling off and reaching over to the clothes rack. I took down one of the white suits I had taken to wearing after the hospital experience.

"Get dressed, wear a mini-skirt. You can fix your make-up in the car."

"Are you wanting me to fuck this guy?"

"No. Get dressed. Now."

She could hear the alacrity in my voice, and see that I was hurrying. So after a brief moment in the washroom, she pulled a denim mini-skirt out of her suitcase and put it on, along with a tight green collared shirt. The green was forest, and there was a moment there when my knees grew weak as she pulled the shirt over her bare breasts.

"Do I have to wear panties?"

"Naw. But listen—"

I went into the bathroom and returned with a tiny vial and a hypodermic syringe with a large gauge needle. I jammed the needle into the top of the vial, and drew its contents into the chamber of the hypo.

"What is that?"

"A barbiturate."

Her eyes were blank.

"Ever heard of truth serum?"

"Uh, yeah—in James Bond movies. That stuff is real?"

"Real as Rioja. It's called sodium pentothal. It works best IV, but this is a huge dose."

I capped the syringe and handed it to her.

"Put it in your purse. Here's how it's gonna go: you sit in the back seat next to the geezer…"

She giggled.

"…I'll be getting into the front passenger side. Waste no time. As soon as you sit down next to him, jam the thing into his thigh and push it all in."

## 9

*A talebearer reveals secrets, but he who is of a faithful spirit conceals a matter.*

*—Proverbs 11*

"Let me piss, I think you knocked something loose!" Lexi laughed and danced into the bathroom. I parted the curtains a little and peeked out. I could just see the roof of Darryl's Corolla, still sitting there in the parking lot. The sun seared my eyes. It was one of those bright, airless, Texas summer days where the sky was so big and empty that it dwarfed you into an introspective insect crawling across a never-ending plain.

If you look at a map, Dallas is plop in the center of the Northeast quadrant of Texas. But in truth, DFW is the borderlands. You will hear it said that Dallas is the last city of the South, and Fort Worth the first city of the West. Drive from

Memphis to El Paso and you will see the geographical truth of that.

That day, the sky over Dallas was arid and Western. Heat waves rose into mirages over East Grand Ave.

"Damn girl, what the hell?" I said at the bathroom door.

"I'm coming! Jeez, I think you really did knock something loose, cowboy."

She bustled out, powdering her nose. She put a compact into her purse.

"I thought I said put your makeup on in the car?"

"Would that be before, or after I stab the pervert with a needle?"

Who can argue with the logic of a nineteen-year-old girl you'd just boned in a motel room? Many have tried and failed. I just opened the door and pushed her out ahead of me. I locked the knob-lock by turning the tab and shut the door behind me. Such was the extent of motel security in 1986. As I stepped into the sun, the air felt as though I had just walked into a furnace. The sharp scent of Lexi's Virginia Slim added to the stifling effect, and I felt sweat beading on my forehead in seconds. Wearing the suit of white had felt right in the room, but now I was regretting not wearing something cooler. I undid the top buttons of my argent shirt. My jacket hid my .38, so I couldn't remove it yet.

I have to give it to Lexi, she didn't seem nervous in the least. I try to remember back on any signs that she'd taken some downers, but it doesn't seem like it. With a girl like her though, who can say? In self-defense, she kept many things hidden—something else she learned from her bastard father. Those were the things about her that I would have been able to ferret out, had my dick not been running interference. Oldest story in the book. For most of us, for some reason, we have to learn which head should be doing the thinking the hard way. For a few, the hard way is a 3x6 box, or a 6x9 cell. I'm one of those few, though I'm not quite sure I ever really learned that one.

The Tampico has more of a pedigree than you would expect of a fleabag motel, and like most structures with any age on them, it has its secrets. Anyone who has stayed or visited the place, or even passed by on East Grand, could see the two main two-story buildings that serve as the motel proper. What few know, few on the right side of the law anyway, is that there was another set of rooms completely invisible from the street; inaccessible except by an insignificant-looking blind alley accessed only by driving through the parking lot and circumnavigating the maintenance shed. These hidden rooms were only occupied by "friends of the ownership." I lived in one of them for over a year while I was on the run for the attempted murder of my parole officer. My food and necessities were brought to me—I never left. I helped them illegally install HBO, which actually brought in quite a bit of money for them, so I don't even think my uncle had to pay rent after a while.

By 1986 I was paying though, and out the ass, because Mr. Knight (the owner) knew I had a shitload of narcotics stashed back there. Never had any trouble out of him though, because we blacks of West Dallas had been supplying Knight's secret little heroin habit for years. If Knight's Italian friends ever found out about his vice, the next thing that would be found (or wouldn't be found) would be Knight's fat body at the bottom of White Rock. The vicious cycle there, and something I still find amusing, was that ninety percent of the heroin coming out of West Dallas back then was being supplied by Knight's Italian bosses.

As Lexi and I stepped from the stairs of the main building onto the pavement of the parking lot, I looked over and noticed that the windows of Darryl's little Toyota were all rolled down, and that the engine wasn't running. I had to spend a moment suppressing a little rage. The interior of his P.O.S.

would be 120 degrees plus. I shook it off and took a look into the back seat. It was Maximilian Parrot alright. His face stared back at me with that familiar brand of suspicion reserved for rich whites against blacks—any blacks. I felt my hackles rise again as the white suspicion's opposite flowed through me. Centuries worth of it. I gained control of myself again, thinking about what I was about to do to this man—and how I was going to spend his money.

I opened the passenger side back door for Lexi and got her in before opening the passenger front and sliding in next to Darryl. Sweat began to pour off me within a second of my ass hitting the scorching seat. Max Parrot chuckled.

"Darryl didn't say nothin' 'bout a monkey in a white suit," Parrot said.

I smiled back at him with hard eyes.

"Pleased to make your acquaintance, Mr. Parrot. I was under the impression that you were interested in making a certain business transaction. It seems I've been misled…"

"Oh no, no, Mr. ah…?"

"Mr. Dick."

Parrot's voice fell flat.

"No, Mr. *Dick*. I'm still very much interested in doing business. Ah…"

"Let's go, Darryl," I said. "Around the shed."

Darryl started the engine. I looked back at Lexi and watched as she cupped Parrot's balls with her left hand, smiling up into his enraptured face. In the same movement, she used her right hand to reach across and jab the big hypo- deep into his skinny thigh, depressing the plunger.

"What the hell was that, bitch!? What the…?"

"Sweet nightmares, asshole."

Parrot conked out with his mouth open. His head lolled back onto Lexi's shoulder. She shoved his dead weight the other way.

"What the hell, E? What are we doing?" Darryl asked, his voice shaky.

"First, we are going around the corner to my private room to get a Polaroid camera and some more dope. Then, we are driving over to the Anchor Inn on Harry Hines where we are going to try our hands at a little amateur photography. We'll wake ol' Max here up just enough to have his eyes open for some shots of his freaky ass naked in bed with a black man and a young girl. We're going to be living in the Bahamas in a month, kids!"

Lexi laughed a throaty laugh that I'll never forget.

"My man is a fucking genius! What, you brought him over to buy some pussy or something, Darryl?"

"Um…yeah," Darryl answered.

I should have told her the truth about Parrot's intentions right then and there, but I figured I had plenty of time for that. And I didn't want complications. *Let her think what she wants.* I stayed silent and pointed Darryl down the blind alley and where to park.

"Where's the briefcase?"

"I—in the back. He had it."

"Lexi, you see a briefcase back there?"

"Yeah. Here it is."

"Bring it. Come on, man. Max is out for a while. He can stay in the car."

We got out of the car and I opened the door to my secret room. My mind was racing. I'd hit the big score. Maybe, if I could pull it off. *No more dealing. No more work. No more running.* Max Parrot was one of the richest motherfuckers in the world! My only problem was figuring out how many millions I could squeeze him for.

Once in the room, I started putting the supplies we'd need together: camera, preludes and coke to wake him up…I said it out loud like I was Julia Childs on freebase—naming off ingredients for a delectable recipe. More barbs to put his stupid ass back down. "Man, even you could pull this off, Darryl."

"What about me, baby?" asked Lexi.

"What?" I said distractedly. "How much is in that briefcase, anyway?"

Darryl was counting it. "Man, E…at least 50 Gs."

I was sitting on the bed, packing, when I felt Lexi's hot breath on my neck.

"What about me?" she whispered.

"What about you, sugar? I told you what we are going to do…"

"You're my best friend, aren't you E?" she said, voice dripping. I hadn't been paying attention. The room we were in had been aglow with *the cream* the entire time. I knew for a split second that something was very, very wrong when I felt Lexi's hand reach around and fondle my cock through my pants, her lips on my ear; then the sharp pinch of a needle as it was jabbed into my neck. I tried to throw her off. "*Bitch!*" I said. Or, I tried to say it. Nothing came out. I fell like a stone.

fi                    fi                    fi

BEEP…………………………………………BEEP……………….
………………BEEP……………………………………BEEP

The dream was like a memory. I remember the water first. Being submerged in it. The warm, slow movement of the waves gently pulling my body. The flavor of salt runs through me like heat. The shimmery sunlight suffuses all about me. There are creatures floating and swimming around my body.

Vague memories run across my thoughts with little hints of understanding, and then slip from my grasp like shadowy, fey beings seen at a distance through the branches of an enchanted wood.

*Move.*

A pressure, a soft command pushes me in a certain direction.

*Move.*

*Up.*

The light of the sun becomes brighter. I shy from it. I can feel myself physically longing for the comfort and safety of the depths.

*No.*

*Move.*

I will myself *up*, focusing on the sparkle of the sun. The closer I get to the surface, the more uncomfortable I become. A deep, anxious thing comes alive in me, a primal fear. It wrestles with my fleeting sense of peace.

*Move.*

I break the surface of the water, and I become part of another world. My senses change, and now I am floating; I am pulled by the waves toward a sandy shore. The sun beams on me as I draw closer and closer to the beach. I can remember my name now, and a brief flash of a woman's glowing face. I feel wet sand on my fingers and arms.

*Move.*

Again, I fight the impulse to use my muscles, or to do anything other than just lie there with the gentle waves pushing at my body. The sun shines redly through the sanguine vessels of my closed eyelids.

*Move.*

Without opening my eyes, I push myself up onto my hands and knees and begin to crawl. The sand of the beach is warm as I move ever so slowly up and away from the rolling sound of the sea. Suddenly, without warning, the flesh of my cheek is pierced by something sharp. I jerk away from the pain and open my eyes to see the threat. The offending thing is a lone, beflowered cactus growing out of the sand. A red drop of my blood hangs from one of its thorns. I glance up and the dazzling sun pierces my brain.

"Aah–aah!" I yelled.

The bright light that had been shone directly into my eyes was withdrawn.

"Oh! Well. Something is happening. He may be waking up," the voice of the speaker was above me.

The second sensation I became aware of, after the brightness, was pain. It was a rough ache in my head that dulled my thoughts. I shut my eyes to the gleam of my surroundings and the darkness helped—a little. My ears became my primary sensory organs, and I forced myself to listen.

BEEP..............................BEEP.......................
..............BEEP.....................................

It was the sound of a hospital machine. I was in a hospital bed. I could still feel the water and the sand between my fingers, but the sensations were fading. I thought of the shock of the thorn piercing my cheek. *That was new. A recurring dream.* The thought bubbled to the surface.

"Mr. Thomas?" said the same voice. "Mr. Thomas, can you hear me? Do you understand?"

I croaked out a quiet "yeah." My eyes stayed shut and my head throbbed with a horrible pain. There was a pressure on my temples, forehead, and behind my ears that felt as if it was going to crack my skull at any moment.

"My name is Dr. Takot, Mr. Thomas."

"Dr. Taco?"

"T–A–K–O–T, the "t" is silent. How do you feel? I'm afraid you are in the ICU at the moment, sir. You've been unconscious for three days."

"Pain," I groaned. "Head."

"Yes," he responded. "I would expect that."

I felt his deft fingers press my eyelids open again and shine the light into my pupils. Waves of agony pressed into my skull as I tried to squirm away from him.

"Nurse," I heard him say in a voice like an echo. "Push four milligrams of morphine now, and four more in ten minutes. Sir, you are recovering from a massive drug overdose. You very nearly died."

A warm sensation suffused my chest, and the pain in my head began to dull. Out of nowhere, the memory of Lexi's Judas kiss came to me—the stab of the needle in my neck. I hurt too bad to think about it. I went off into a daze. I opened my eyes what seemed only a moment later at the sound of someone at my bedside.

"Here's your second dose." It was a nurse carrying a syringe. Her nametag read: *Beatrice, Parkland Hospital*. She plunged the clear liquid into my IV. Comfort settled into my spine and I felt myself drifting into unconsciousness. I tried to turn over in the bed and realized that my left leg was shackled to the rail. I took a deep breath and willed myself to taste the salty water of my dream.

## 10.

I feel like I've been placed in a little cell at the center of a crossroads where time doesn't pass, but instead, is always at the moment just before the sun crests the horizon. At first, I would look in vain at the lightened sky—sure in my knowledge that the sun was on the verge of crossing the threshold. Or that some person, or group, or vehicle would be shortly coming into view, going any direction on either of the roads. After a while the truth becomes clear. Time itself is taken. Stolen. Or I had lost it. Even the crickets I hear in the distance cheep one long, incessant note. With that knowledge, the comprehension of my own timeless place comes the fear. And the fear has grown into a mortal dread.

Despite the evidence gathered by my senses, the movement of my thoughts and the changes in my feelings teach me another truth: Inside, some clock still ticks. And now I gaze along the roads, and the glowing horizon, with another kind of expectancy altogether. The shining white rider of salvation once hoped for has become Death on his pale horse.

Eben came into the tank on a Sunday. They have fancy doors in the West Tower. There are two buttons high on the inner steel frame in a stainless panel with four tiny holes punched for a microphone, and six concentric rings of the same sized holes punched for a speaker. The panel is about 3 ½ inches wide and 8 inches tall. Above the top button is printed **CALL**, and below the bottom is **DOOR**. From breakfast until rack time, at either midnight on weeknights or one in the morning on weekends, the **DOOR** button is backlit with a traffic-light green, which tells you that it is active.

On that Sunday, the green of the light caught my eye as it came alive. It was a shock of bright color among the ubiquitous browns and off-whites of the cell. I saw the inmate workers with their carts full of breakfast trays, their guard-handlers holding sheaves of paper: printouts of inmate names with special medical diets highlighted. They were feeding 11 tank, which was around the corner at an inside angle from our tank, number 1. They were about to move on to 12 tank, and then they would be to us. I sat and listened attentively to my right, toward C cell. All was quiet.

I dozed and was then jolted awake moments later by the crank of the doors rolling open.

"Chow time! Chow time!" The old character who had been watching the *Partridge Family* was being kind enough to wake everyone up for chow with his annoying-ass voice. He was a cackler and a crackhead; basically good-natured, but with an I.Q. somewhere southerly of 75. With as many of them as there are in the system, I have learned to treat his kind more gently. Their crimes are generally those of social annoyance: vagrancy, trespassing, petty theft, and public intox. From the inside, it feels as though society was locking up people in wheelchairs because they found themselves unable to walk like the rest of us. The ugliness of it all chokes me.

Yeah, I'll tell his kind to fuck off on occasion, but these people are prey to a certain kind of predator who exists one rung above them on the food chain: the grade-school bullies reenacting their petty, vicious youths in jail—full of anger and frustration that they hadn't been crowned kings of their world, and feel as if they should have been already, by rights.

I watched as this specimen yelled "chow time!" and knocked on cell windows. I saw him approach C cell and knock, pause, and then beat insistently.

"What?" came from behind the door.

"You gonna eat?"

"No…and don't wake me up again, asshole."

"A'ight," came the response with a cackle. "Sleep late, lose weight!"

"Lose this," Eben replied.

The cackler glanced into my cell, but seeing me awake and attentive he gave me an idiot grin in response to the smile I was wearing in amusement at Eben's attitude. The cackler spun on his heel and yelled again, "Chow time! Sleep late, lose weight! He he he!"

I stood up and pressed my **DOOR** button. The door to my cell wheezed and popped open as the trustees started shoving trays through the bean chute. Walking to one of the tank's two four-seater tables, tray in hand, I risked a glance into C cell. The man was wrapped in his sheet and facing the wall. His glow had yet to fade, and I caught myself cutting looks as I choked down my diet tray. The tank ate in silence with the exception of the cackler, who was able to snag the extra tray. He chortled at his luck. I was overwhelmed by the sense that rather than watching a grown man, I was watching a small child who

47

had been presented with a new toy, or a squirrel that had stumbled upon a secret trove of its favorite nuts. "He he he!"

As my cellmates drifted off to their respective cages, after dropping their trays through the bean chute for the inmate workers to clean up, I finally dropped off my own tray and went to my cell. I quietly made myself a John Wayne. I sipped at it and thumbed through a dog-eared copy of a Franz Kafka book that I had found by small miracle on the book cart two weeks before.

Sleep overtook me. I translated over into unconsciousness from one word to the next. I awoke to the sound of the television playing quietly. I recognized the program as being a late Sunday morning PBS show. Bill Moyers. I listened with my eyes closed as he spoke about income disparities in Silicon Valley: How the middle class population there in the mecca of the Internet had been pushed into poverty by the success of the corporations. I knew a little about such things; I had studied the tenets of black liberation theology. I had enough understanding of wealth and economics to know which side of the debate I was on, though I never engaged in it. Who really cares about the political opinions of a mentally ill, black felon? That's three strikes too many for the political class.

Drifting in disparate thought, I finally opened my eyes to see my new cellmate sitting at the near table. He was sipping coffee and watching the Moyers program. *What's this?* I thought to myself. *The cream*, my gift, my curse—it burned in my belly. Often when the religious commit their souls to God, they are told, "Now your life is no longer your own, it belongs to Another." This is usually an abstract idea, an expression of the movement from self-will to God-will. But for me, it was all too real. Whoever or whatever had created this feeling of affinity had given me little choice in the matter of what I was to do with it.

The man glanced at me over the rim of his cup as he took a sip, and then looked back over at his show. He was letting me know that he was aware of my eyes studying him. He was in his early thirties and in good physical condition. He was about six feet in height and not more than 180 pounds. His hair was cut short, as if buzzed with a three-guard. He was dark of eye, and held himself with an animalistic grace that seemed natural. His– animalness was not an uncommon sight, especially in prison proper. Almost one hundred percent of the time I'd run into such a jailhouse archetype, especially in white men, their image was incomplete without numerous grey and black prison style tattoos, yet he had none. I couldn't see his legs or torso, but something told me he had not a single tattoo—jailhouse or otherwise.

Upon the second time he looked over at me, I had no choice but to get up and join him at the table. Horrible violence often began with one man staring at another. I stood non-threateningly and spooned some more instant coffee into my cup. I noticed that there was now a hot pot plugged into the wall. He must have brought it in. I pushed my green button and stepped out into the dayroom. He did not turn, but kept his eyes on his program. We shared the room alone. Our six other cellmates were likely asleep.

"Mind if I use a little of that water?" I asked him.

"Sure," he responded. "Just fill it up if you use it all, if you don't mind."

I walked over to the brown shelf that hung under the TV near the outlet for just such a purpose, and filled my cup with steaming water. I raised the cup to my nose and luxuriated in the aroma of the instant coffee. I'd stopped drinking brewed since my most recent stint. Eight calendar years in California, from '99 to '07.

"Ahhh, hot fucking coffee. Thank you."

"No problem, man," he said, focus on the Moyers show. I looked up at it. Moyers had a Native American writer named Sherman Alexie on. He was reading from his poetry book called *Blasphemy*. He read a shocking poem about Lincoln. According to the poem—and Alexie as he expanded upon the subject—on the day before signing the emancipation proclamation, Lincoln signed the orders for the largest execution in U.S. history. Thirty-eight Indians were ordered to be executed for their part in some insurrection. Most likely they had the audacity to make a claim on the land their people had been living on for hundreds, if not thousands, of years. One of them was pardoned at the last moment, but the other thirty-seven were stretched.

"That son of a bitch," my new neighbor said, voice thick with emotion. He looked over at me. "That fucking son of a bitch." No tears fell, but his eyes were wet.

"My name is Eben, bro," he told me.

"Ezekiel. They call me Preacher Man."

"And you know what?" said Eben. "Nothing's changed. Not a thing. I had a cellie a few weeks back over in the South Tower- his name was Louis. He did two tours in Afghanistan and one in Iraq. He was Army, Airborne.

"We got to talking about the wars—man, he was a staff sergeant, I believe, but what it boiled down to was, especially on his first tour, which was the initial strike on Afghanistan in '02, that his job was to parachute down onto a roof in a village with a monster machine gun—what are they? .50 caliber? And just start pumping lead into the houses. The detail that got me was how he described actually aiming the gun and pulling the trigger down in measured bursts into each little hut. From what he said, how they did it was to hold down the trigger and say, 'family of eight' then shift to the next hut, 'family of eight'… Ratattatatt… What it meant was that this was a burst that was long enough to kill a family of eight. He knew he was killing kids too. They all did."

"How did he get locked up?" I asked him. Shimmers of *the cream* surrounded Eben like an aura. I felt as though I was both watching and participating in some grand play, reciting and enraptured by its lines.

"That's part of it too," Eben went on. "Apparently, juice– steroids was a huge problem over there. It was so common that almost every one of Louis's buddies was doing it— working out, getting big. And the officers not only let it go, they fucking approved it! Can you guess why? What's one of the main side effects of anabolic steroids? Rage. 'Roid rage. A buddy of mine used and sold them years ago. He was some kind of amateur body builder, I don't know, but I ended up hating it, getting around that guy. He was constantly on the edge of an explosion. It got to where he would just walk into a bar, sit down, and call somebody a bitch just to start a fight. No alcohol, just straight juice."

"So what," I asked him, "he came back over here and got busted for steroids?"

"No. It gets worse."

The Moyers Show had ended. Eben stood and manipulated the buttons on the TV, which was locked onto a metal swivel-shelf attached to the wall about seven feet from the floor. He flipped the channel over to 3, which was the jail station. Basically the radio. They put on various local stations over videos of public messages such as "The address for the Public Defender's Office is…" or, "If you feel you are in jail by mistaken identity, please contact the control center immediately." The radio was on a pop station. Eben turned the volume down to the level of background noise.

"You good on coffee?" he asked me.

"Yeah, thanks." I replied.

"Preacher Man, right?" he turned.

"That's what they call me."

He stepped into his cell and spooned coffee into his cup. He poured some hot water and replaced the hot pot onto the shelf. He sipped his coffee and remained standing.

"Worse?" I prompted.

"Much worse. See, they've got all these kits over there. Food, med packs; remedies for this and that. Well, apparently, one of the things the army was concerned about over there was sarin gas: the Nazi shit. Nerve gas. Nasty stuff. Kills in minutes. How they combat it in the field is by these injectable syrettes of what is called phenyl-2-propanol or p2p. It looks like you've done a little time. I'm sure you've heard the schitzers talk about p2p before. It's a choice ingredient in the making of a certain kind of methamphetamine. It's hardly used anymore because it has become so hard to find. I think they used to extract it from certain types of camera film. If you are curious, find an old meth head. He will tell you more than you ever wanted to know. This pharmaceutical grade p2p that the army uses is pure speed. It counters the effects of the nerve gas. With repeated doses, it gives the poisoned soldier a chance to get the medical attention he would need to survive. From what Louis said, this shit was everywhere—especially in Iraq during the early stages of the invasion. Jeez, have you heard that combat vets are committing suicide at the rate of twenty-two a day? *Twenty-two a day!* After talking to Louis, I'm not surprised at all."

Eben continued, "Louis and his buddies started in on using the p2p recreationally. He really blew my mind with this story, man; especially with the way he told it. He wasn't trying to open my eyes to the horrors of war, or make some political statement. Hell, he told me several times that he wished he could go back, even though he was completely burnt out. PTSD toast. No, if anything, he was seeking some kind of approbation. It was buried deep beneath jaded, defensive eyes—but it was there. I offered what comfort I could.

"At the same time, I'd gotten these visions of trained killers, equipped with the most advanced armaments in the world, juiced up, rushing on pharmaceutical speed, made to hate the enemy, turned loose to kill and do damage. He said they would play heavy metal songs like "Let the Bodies Hit the Floor" during combat ops. Even if isolated, this was a travesty. I got the sense, however, that this was simply the way of things over there, swallowed up by the fog of war. These kinds of experiences would turn anyone's brain into a psychiatric experiment gone wrong. After coming back home, he couldn't assimilate back to normal life. He stabbed his wife in a panic attack, and their relationship eventually broke apart. He wound up hooking back up with a buddy from the war, and one day his buddy said, 'Hey, remember that p2p shit we were doing over there?'

'Yeah,' said Louis.

'Well hey, this is basically the same thing.'

"His buddy pulled out a glass pipe with a little bulb on the end of it and handed it over to Louis.

'Just suck in real lightly, and turn the pipe in your thumb and forefinger between 10 and 2. I'll light it up,' his friend told him.

"It was meth, of course. Common, modern, Mexican ice. And Louis loved it. He and his buddies got together and started a little sales venture with the shit. And you know the end of the story, Mr. Preacher. A year or so later, Louis got pulled over in his truck—he was totally spun. He said they found a pound and a half of meth and twelve thousand in cash. The kicker is that by the time he was booked in, the evidence paperwork said he was charged with eight ounces and $2,000! He said he remembered one of the cops saying, 'hey, I'm going to do us both a favor, buddy!' and laughing. Of course, he didn't breathe a word. That dropped his charges down an entire degree. How many times have you heard *that* story in jail? War

53

on Drugs, my ass. I think he said he ended up signing for seven years. That's American justice for you in a nutshell, unless you want to add that if he'd been black, he'd have gotten shot when he was arrested." Eben laughed.

"Wow. What a story," I said.

I said that because I lacked the words to express what I truly felt at that moment. The story of Louis was compelling enough, but it was the telling of it that had struck me dumb. Eben had the knack of throwing his voice into some primal place in me. What's more, I felt rearrangements, movements, and openings in me: *the cream*. The beginnings of an exchange were being made between this Eben and myself. Eben Thomas. I'd glanced down at his wristband—the one we are all required to wear that identifies us by name, number, race, birthdate, housing location, and barcode. Eben *Thomas*. I registered the strangeness that was the fact that we shared the same last name. Like everything else about the man, it threw me off balance. I had a vague notion that my views and beliefs about the world were under attack by a subtle foe. A part of me, a strong part, wanted to get up from the table and end all of this before it had well and truly begun. Was that a choice within my power to make? I don't know. I like to believe that I have at least some control over what I do, whom I interact with. I can choose to pick up my hand right now and stop writing. Or can I? Certainly you could stop reading this account at the end of this sentence —perhaps it would be better for your overall mental health if you did. Or *could* you stop? The scientists talk about determinism—the lack of free will—but I think they are missing the soul forest for the mechanical trees. Einstein said, "God does not play dice." He was right, but for the wrong reasons. It's not God, it's the devil playing the dice. I've seen him down in West Dallas shooting craps with the boys on a concrete slab. His laugh is like a hyena's at dusk on an open plain.

I sat and contemplated what was going on inside me. I felt memories tumbling over and through one another. *The cream* itself had become such that my vision was not as it had been. *The cream* had usually manifested itself as a dilation of time, wherein a sense in my mind could tease out hints of things that were hidden. This was something else. I've taken LSD three times, and those experiences are the only things that remotely compare. Without the confusion, though, just...it was overwhelming. I was overwhelmed by a sensation of *otherness*. As I explored the feeling further, I realized that something else was different about this exchange: A thousand times in my life, at the least, I sat across from another human being and knew that what transpired between us was more, much more, than a conversation, a prayer, sex—I have no doubt in my mind that these were mystical transactions. I don't have the least bit of concrete evidence to prove my beliefs; I simply know that they are the truth. Many of those who shared in these experiences would agree. Most of them would confess a sense that something odd was happening; the religious would connect the experience with their faith, hence my name "Preacher Man."

This man sitting before me though, *he knew*. And most unsettling of all, I got the sense that he knew more or better than did I concerning this transaction. A dulled dread settled over my shoulders and wrapped itself around my neck.

Eben and I were sitting across from each other at the steel table; both of us perched on the round stools connected to the table's base. An enterprising inmate from some other day/month/year had etched a chessboard into the paint of the table. It was incorrect: the black corner squares on the right instead of on the left, as they should be. Nevertheless, I appreciated the effort, as well as the effort of the kid in G cell, a hardheaded youngster named Mason, who had fashioned the tank some chess pieces out of toilet paper. He had wet the paper and then let them dry in shape—dyeing the black pieces with cherry cool-aid. It was a beautiful set, all in all, and correctly set up for a match on the reversed board. Eben was closer to being behind the white side. He idly reached out and moved the queen pawn out to his fourth rank.

"So Eben...ah," I began, "what are you in for?"

Under normal circumstances, this is not a question you would ask another inmate before you got to know them well. If they wanted you to know, they would tell you. But I felt compelled. Eben met my gaze before he spoke.

## Part II: Raven a Harbinger

*As for the appearance of their faces: the four had the face of a human being, the face of a lion on the right side, the face of an ox on the left side, and the face of an eagle; such were their faces.*

—*Ezekiel 1*

# 11.

"Alright, I'll tell you. My story begins at one of my old hangouts. Have you ever heard of the club Two-Four?"

"Ah…" I responded. "Yeah. It's a half-way house over in Old East Dallas, right?"

"Club Two-Four, also known simply as 'the Two-Four,' is a half-way house located in the oldest section of East Dallas, over on Ross Avenue. It inhabits a huge, old, manse of a building; decades ago when it was founded, it was in a much more modestly sized house closer to lower Greenville Ave. It originated as a twelve-step club for drunks on skid row to have a safe place to dry out. As the twelve-step idea of drunks and drug addicts helping each other get sober picked up momentum, the Club Two-Four became a crossroads for the drunk, the newly sober, and the long sober. Before long, some clever administrator of the establishment decided that it would be a grand idea to open the kitchen of the place up to the public. This changed the front meeting area into a diner, and popularity increased until it was eventually able to live up to its name and remain open twenty-four hours a day.

"You can stroll up to the huge front porch of the Two-Four at just about any given moment of the day or night and be confronted by a diverse assortment of dope-fiends, alkies, crackheads, junkies, misfits, ex-cons, bikers, Iranians, and mental patients of every stripe and color. It was somewhere around the vernal equinox. As it often is in Texas in spring, the temperature was in the mid-sixties. As my good friend, Harry the Indian (he was some kind of an Apache I believe), and I walked up the sidewalk from the parking lot of the place, I felt the warm inner comfort that goes along with the feeling of belonging.

"There were probably twenty, maybe twenty-five men and women outside, and the conversation was as heavy as the cigarette smoke. All of the usual suspects were present. On my left, a new, young and pretty meth-whore was tittering uncomfortably at the poor jokes of two men in their mid-fifties who, I am sure, believed their dirty intentions were well hidden. I chuckled to myself as I watched one of the more matronly women of the club casually step over and rescue the girl, who suddenly took on the look of someone who was very unsure as to why she was there. On our right, sitting cheek to cheek on one of the rough wooden benches and laughing wholeheartedly as if it were the most natural thing in the world, was a tall, ponytailed man in full rebel biker regalia, a man dressed to the nines in an expensive business suit—dark blue silk tie still in place, and a man who looked as though he had been pulled out from the bottom of a dumpster only moments before. Harry naturally veered towards the three, they were close friends of his—mere acquaintances of mine, as were most of the club goers, though I'd known many of them for over a year by then. No one had seen James, the man in bum garb, for months. Harry brightened when his weak eyes found him.

"Harry was, by orders of magnitude, more popular, social, and openly mentally deranged than I was, so he took the lead. He was addressed first, anyway, as we stepped up onto the porch.

"'Chicago!' Harry called to ponytail.

"'Harry! You crazy Indian!' Chicago responded. The three stood.

"'You fucking hooker,' Harry said with a huge smile that showed his gleaming, white dentures. The dentures were too big for his mouth, but everyone could remember when Harry's teeth were an absolute wreck.

"'Fuck you too, Steve!' Harry addressed the man in the suit, who grinned back with teeth that were perfect and real.

"'And whoo-hoo! Look what dragged the cat in!' You could smell James from five feet away, but Harry stepped in with his smallish Indian frame and wrapped the filthy man in a hug.

"'I love you, brother,' he said. 'I don't care if you stay sober, or not. I love you just the same. I want you to know it.'

"'Thank you, Harry.' Wetness stood in red eyes. 'Thank you,'

"Harry reached into his jacket pocket and took out his cigarette pack. He took out about half of what he had left and handed them to James.

"'Don't smoke 'em all at once, dumb fuck.'

"'What's up, fellas?' I said to the three.

"'Eben,' Chicago replied, shaking my hand. Steve nodded to me, and James croaked out a 'Hey.'

"We stood around while Harry and Chicago traded insults—long enough for Harry to finish his smoke. He threw his butt in an old coffee can on our way inside and toward the dining area."

Eben paused his narrative.

"I suppose you are intelligent and perceptive enough to realize why I was there? Why these people were my friends?"

Eben drained his coffee. He spooned more out of his bag and into his cup and poured more hot water.

"You're an alcoholic," I said.

"Well," he went on, "I suppose I am. Likely I am, at least. Folks say that if you get addicted to one type of recreational chemical, you may as well be addicted to all of them. I don't know. You are close enough. The reason I was at the Two-Four is my love affair with opiates. Painkillers. Specifically Roxicodone, but any opioid would do in a pinch. A few successive, tragic events in my life led me to the Two-Four in the spring of last year, desperate and haggard. Harry was doing at least half-assed with his problems at the time, and he was there on the porch of the place when I straggled up the sidewalk, looking for I don't know what. He asked me what the fuck was I doing there—just like that, no preamble, and I informed him about exactly where he could shove his questions and what was he going to do if he didn't like it. We immediately became friends. One of my first experiences at the Two-Four, later that evening, was to watch Harry get up behind the podium, in front of at least fifty people, and proceed to babble like a madman. I was shocked when another man, I think his name was Terry, got up, handed Harry a little round medallion, and congratulated him for staying sober an entire year. *Must have been last year*, I thought to myself.

"The experience was sufficiently strange enough to keep me hanging around the place; I made a few more friends, or near-friends. I've been a loner since high school days—being on a first name basis with a person was going out on a social limb for me. I even took a few stabs at getting sober, half-hearted as they were. I knew in my bones that sobriety just wasn't in the cards for me. The idea of it was attractive, though. I wanted to be near sobriety. If you know much about addiction, you'll understand that there is no paradox there. And that's the how and why of my coming to love the Two-Four and its people, in my distant, dark way.

"Leaving our three friends on the porch, we went into the diner and over to the little window where one of the halfway-house's residents was taking orders and cooking.

"'Two large coffees and two of the hubcap pancakes, man,' I ordered.

"'Four fifty,' he replied.

"I dug out a five and a one and handed it over to the man, who wore a hairnet. I'd seen him a hundred times before, but I didn't have a clue as to what his name was. 'Keep it,' I said. 'Over my shoulder,' Harry said, 'Hey Chad, workin' hard back there?'

"'*Oh yeah*,' I thought, '*Chad*.'

"'Same old shit, Harry. You good tonight?'

"'Wishing I was a couple feet deep in some pussy right about now, but other than that I'm blessed.'

"We all laughed as I poured the creamer and sugar into our large, Styrofoam cups full of steaming coffee. Harry and I turned and found a table. There were maybe ten other people, mostly familiar faces, sitting by themselves or in twos and threes scattered about the dining area.

"I was functional at the time, if barely. What I mean is that I had a ride, a place to stay, clean clothes, and I was able to support a mild Roxi habit by holding together a ring of old crackheads that I had

hitting the doctors for scripts. This was a balancing act of monumental proportions that involved buying and selling crack, buying and selling pussy, occasionally punching crackheads in the face while I'm driving them to a doctor or pharmacy, selling Roxi to lawyers, businessmen, hookers, hair stylists, you name it —all of which I had to be high to deal with. And man, I hated it. I was desperately trying to find a way out that I could swing without too much pain.

"Harry was the only person at the Two-Four that I could talk to. He was the only one who knew the truth about what I had going on. He'd proved long before that I could trust him, and beyond that—he was dying. He was barely fifty years old, but his liver and his kidneys were shot to hell. On a few occasions since I had known him his health had nearly failed, and he'd had to spend days or weeks at a time in the hospital.

"While we were finding our seats and sitting down, a dark-haired—but not black-haired—girl named Raven was taking an acoustic guitar out of its case and sitting on a stool over by the old fireplace. Raven was a resident at the Two-Four and a nightmarishly bad alcoholic. She was in her late twenties, and had been a folk singer of note around the bars and clubs of East Dallas for several years. This made her alcohol problem difficult to solve, considering she was known and loved by every barkeep and every regular at every nearby bar.

"Raven was beautiful—shockingly so. I'd been attracted to her since the day we met. She flashed a smile at me, and I returned it before she strummed the guitar and started to sing:

> I am sitting in this....
> Here behind the…
> Hands neatly…

"As if he'd been waiting for the background music, Harry turned his wild eyes onto me, gazing in, and spoke.

"'Eben, we need to talk,' he said.

"'What'sup,Harry?'

"'Well,' Harry leaned in closer to me, and while I was looking at him his outer edges became lined with an other-worldly light. It was as if he were throwing some kind of radiation that was so powerful it was bleeding over into the visual spectrum.

"Slowly, trying to keep from drawing attention to myself, I reached into my inside jacket pocket and snagged the emergency Roxi that I kept loose and within reach at all times. I popped it and took a sip of coffee, knowing that I'd probably be showing some signs of intoxication before it would be time for me to leave the Two-Four, but this was why I'd started taking the pills in the first place. I knew I was crazy. I experienced visual hallucinations. I still do, in case you are wondering. Don't worry, I've never snapped and gone psycho or anything. Even without my pills, it hasn't been all that bad. At least until…um, anyway…no, not too bad. When I started seeing things, I had to take more pills. If nothing else in my world made sense, they did. As Harry spoke and his body sparked, I was okay with it because I knew that in just a few minutes the rush of the mind– and soul-numbing painkiller would ease my fear and lessen the feeling that I was spinning out of control.

"Harry reacted to my taking the pill only by pausing and glancing down as I popped it.

"'Eben,' Harry went on, 'you know how I told you about how I used to talk to the spirit?'

"'Um…yeah, I ah…'

"'Those were dark days for me, Eben. Days that had no sun. Those were the days that I died…where I found my death, you understand?'     "I didn't really. But the question was rhetorical.     "'I asked the spirits questions,' he said, 'and they answered. But I paid for those answers with my sanity and my health, you understand?' He chuckled for a moment; his laugh was so incongruous with his words that I stared at him in shock. His craziness had sparked my own, and I was losing myself in it.

"'It wasn't so long ago, you know,' he went on, 'but in order to survive I closed myself to them, ran from them. I've been running ever since.'

"I could feel the Roxi stabilizing my nerves. A warmth

was building in my belly—my arms, my fingers and my spine were tingling in opioid bliss. Even so, the sparks jumping from Harry's body were intensifying. I was falling into a mesmeric state.

"'Until last night,' Harry said.

"'Last night?' I asked. I was having trouble keeping focus.

"'Last night the spirit returned to me, and do you know what she spoke of, Eben? She spoke of you.'

"'*She* spoke of me.'

"'Yes, Eben. Both a blue spirit and a red spirit spoke to me of you, and they both told me the same thing but in differing ways. Differing languages. They told me to give you a warning, for a crossroads comes before you on the path, and you will be forced to choose.'

"I could hear Raven's voice along with her music. It intertwined with Harry's words as they penetrated my skull. As he spoke, I could feel the spirits. One was Raven's guitar, the other her voice: the red alternating with the blue.

"'They told me,' Harry intoned, 'that you will be offered the knowledge that you have sought, and that you will accept it, but that you will be required to pay a price for this knowledge. Once you have accepted this knowledge, you will be given a choice in payment. This choice will be between taking of one of two paths...'

"Harry's voice softened, and he leaned even closer to me. Raven's music steadied into a slow, even rhythm.

"'The easier path, they said, was to the left, and it leads you to death. The more difficult path was to the right, and *it* leads to betrayal. You will have to choose.'

"Harry leaned back in his chair. I stared at him as the sparks around his body faded and became tiny tendrils of blue wisp.

"'This is a little too much for me right now, man,' I said

to him as I stood up on wobbly legs. The Roxi was coming on strong. 'I've gotta get outta here,' I said. 'You can have my pancake.'

"On the spur of the moment, I looked over at Raven as she was strumming random chords on her Taylor acoustic. I stepped over to her and placed my hand over the fret board of the guitar, muffling the sound.

"'Hey,' I said, looking into eyes that still seemed lost in a song. 'You wanna go…somewhere? Other than here?'

"She smiled up at me in a way that told me it had been a very good idea for me to invite her out.

"'Can I carry your guitar?' I said.

"She carefully placed her guitar in its case and snapped shut the fasteners. She looked at me and said, 'just a sec,' before disappearing through the door I knew led to the rooms where the female residents were housed. Not for the first time, I noticed her walk, her shy grace. My eyes followed her slim form bending in its movements.

"I'd seen Raven turn men away so often that my fear of rejection had never allowed me to do more than broach the issue of romance with her in my mind. I'd known the girl for years, but we were friends only by virtue of proximity—never really becoming close. Our personalities were both somewhere on the scale between reserved and withdrawn. While I would sit and listen to her play, I would rarely speak to her after she was finished. I could tell that people made her uncomfortable, which was something I understood. So while others crowded her on account of her music and beauty, I gave her space— choosing not to add to her discomfort, which would have in turn added to my own.

"Standing there and waiting for her to return, I began to feel self-conscious. The Club Two-Four was a building full of alcoholics and drug addicts ostensibly trying to straighten out, many under the threat of dire consequences. Being high could not be easily hidden from such folk—especially not as high as I could feel myself getting. I picked up Raven's guitar and with anxiety looked for her towards the female room. *C'mon Raven, damn.*

"She appeared with a punk rock backpack slung over one shoulder. She was wearing a pair of faded denim blue jeans that fit her form well enough to make me catch a breath. Her top was a stretchy black material that molded itself over her full breasts. She had done something with her face—her *eyes*. She had done something with her make-up, mascara I guess, that emphasized her eyes. This was the Raven that would get up on stage at Poor David's and dazzle audiences with her dark folk songs. I stared as she walked up to me and stopped. She was 5'10" easily, and with the heels on her boots she was eye to eye with me. She smiled.

"'You ready, cowboy?' she said.

"'Let's go.'

"She led the way and as I turned to follow her out I noticed that Harry was still sitting at our table. He had already polished off one of the giant pancakes and was cutting into the other. Even through the haze of the Roxi, it unsettled me to see that I was still hallucinating. Harry's head shined in a pale blue light. He noticed me looking and grinned around a mouthful.

"'Wanna bite?' he asked me. I chuckled at him.

"'See you 'round, Harry,' I said as I passed him. I was almost at the door when I heard him call out.

"'Hey, Eben!'

"I half-turned.

"'Say your prayers, motherfucker,' he said with a straight face, blue light flaring.

"'Thanks, Harry.' I hurried out after Raven, ill at ease."

69

## 12

"**M**y car was a black, 4-door, Honda Accord. It was parked in the lot behind the Two-Four. By the time I caught up with her, Raven had nearly reached it. I fumbled in my pants pocket for the key-chain and pressed the little button that unlocked the doors. I opened the passenger door for Raven before opening the rear door and sliding her guitar case into the seat. I got into the car and started the engine, turned to Raven and looked at her face. She seemed calm, but the thumb and forefinger of her right hand were nervously rubbing the hem of her top.

"'So, uh…' I began.

"'I know you are fucked up, Eben,' she interrupted.

"'Um, I ah…' I was at a loss. She put her finger on my lips to shush me.

"'I wanna get fucked up, too,' she said. 'Let's go to the Stray Light.'

"Perhaps because we had met at the Two-Four and had never drank or gotten high together, I felt obliged to ask her if she wanted to do this. Even though, as an addict, I knew well that the question *Are you sure?* wasn't only stupid, it was utter nonsense under the circumstances—an absurdity. She answered, as I deserved:

"'I don't know, Eben. Maybe you are right. I have these three caps of pure Molly here. I was kinda thinking I'd take one, give you one, and we could split the third unless we happen to run into one of my girlfriends and she wants to hang out. In that case, I'd give *her* the extra cap and we'd take it from there. That, or I could open this door, and my guitar and I could mosey back on in to the Two-Four, I guess…'

"She put her hand on the door handle and looked at me with a sort of crooked smile that only a beautiful woman could pull off without looking silly. I stared in shock as her icy, blue irises began to glow in the darkness of my car. I shivered.

"'Well?' she asked. 'If we are going, let's move. I wanna down this cap with a beer.'

"I put the car in reverse.

"Raven's choice was the Straylight. Club Straylight was maybe five miles from the Two-Four, as the crow flies. It was in a hipster district called Exposition Park, which can be found just over the western border of the sprawling State Fairgrounds. I knew the place. One of my Roxi customers had a storefront in Exposition a few doors down from Straylight. What made the place distinctive was that every conceivable surface, inside and out, was plastered, covered, and inset with thousands of LEDs: the future of design lighting. LEDs are still pricey to install, but once they are up and running you can look like Las Vegas for about as much as it costs to run your dishwasher.

"I was thinking about light and electricity as I drove my Honda through old East Dallas toward our destination. I noticed that Raven had plugged her phone into the auxiliary jack of my stereo and was kicked back in her seat with her eyes closed, listening intently to obscure and abstract atmospheric music. I glanced at the display screen of her phone and caught part of a name, something 'Leaf.'

"There was little traffic on the circuitous route I took that wound its way underneath I-30, down a backstreet, and then up into the dark lot behind the buildings of Exposition Park. Raven opened her backpack and withdrew a lipstick. She flipped the visor down and applied the red tint. I watched intently.

"'Let's do this,' she said after she finished.

"We stepped out of the car and were confronted with the dank scent of some very skunky, potent marijuana. I noticed three fashionably dressed young partiers leaning against a brick wall. Their shadows were stark, thrown by the orange-yellow of the sulfur streetlamps. We passed them. They looked at us with glassy eyes. 'Hey,' one said. We walked through a dark alley and emerged near the doors of Straylight. The *thump–thump–thump* of the dance music hit my body first, then my ears—treble and mids increasing and fading as the doors opened and closed behind comers and goers. Outside stood about fifteen folks in twos and threes, all but one or two holding cigarettes—arms wrapped around bodies to combat the chill early-spring air.

"Through the vibrating windows, I could see LEDs in spidery webs draped over what appeared to be black velvet cloth. Atop the cloth was a bizarre spread of old toys, dolls and figurines of various types, and in various states of distress and disrepair. The shifting colors of the LEDs made the toys appear to move, their shadows shifting ever so slightly as the locus of intensity traveled through one vector and across another.

"Two muscled and tattooed bouncers stood guard, arms crossed, on either side of the doors.

"'Hey boys,' Raven said as we passed between them.

"''Sup, Raven,' one of them responded.

"'Hey Pham,' Raven said to the short but athletic looking Vietnamese collecting cover charges in the hallway just inside. He had on a necklace hung with glow sticks and he moved to the rhythm in an understated dance. It didn't surprise me that he let us in without paying. Clearly, Raven was well known. The first room we came upon was the main bar and dance area. It was full of movement, darkness, shifting light, and intense music. Two DJs were set up in one corner behind a glass partition. LEDs were *everywhere*—set in the floors, the walls, the ceilings; the tables. They hung down in strings like thin stalactites in a flashing cavern. All conceivable colors were present, but reds and greens were predominant. I thought about the amount of work involved in keeping such a display going. *Too much.* It was a true spectacle. It paid off, though, because the place was packed with folk. There were hundreds in the main room, shoulder to shoulder. The bar was surrounded by drinkers eager to slam down another redheaded slut, or shot of Patron, or Jager—all at premium prices.

"Being in such a jumble of humanity was not my cup of tea. Even under the protection of the Roxi, I could feel anxiety constricting my chest and throat.

"Raven leaned in and shouted into my ear, 'We're going to the back!'

"I followed her through the throngs to the other side of the room where she pushed a piece of the wall that opened upon a tube corridor decorated with a spiral design of LEDs. The corridor led to a smaller, quieter bar area where every view was obstructed by huge leather-cushioned booths and oddly placed dividers. I had never been this deep into Straylight before. When we reached the cozy bar, I looked up and realized that I knew the bartender.

"'George!' I said. 'Damn, it's been awhile.'

"'How you doin', Eben?' he replied with a grin that showed his silvery false tooth. 'Raven. Your usual?'

"Raven's usual was Jager bombs: Jagermeister and Red Bull. As George pushed the shots and beers over to us, I noticed that he wrote something on a napkin and handed it to Raven. She slipped it into her pocket without looking at it.

"'Let me just finish my beer first, okay?' she said to George. She smiled up at me; her beauty penetrated the effects of the Roxi. She was possessed of grace and experience, but was still youthful enough to be breathtaking.

"'Well,' she said, 'here we are, here's my beer...' She reached down and pulled a plastic make-up case out of her back pocket. She popped it open to reveal three fat, translucent capsules that were about the size of a multi-vitamin. Each was filled with shiny crystals. She held the case out to me as if offering an Altoids, and I plucked one of the capsules. She took another and put it in her mouth, washing it down with a gulp of her beer—some local craft beer called Naked Truth, which gave me pause. I put my cap under my nose and took a whiff. It was the nasty, unmistakable smell of MDMA—the real thing. I hadn't taken much ecstasy since the days of the H-bomb wafers in the late nineties, but I knew that there was plenty of fake garbage being put on the streets recently.

"'That shit right there is the business, sugar. Pure Molly,' Raven assured me.

"I popped it into my mouth and washed it down. I lifted my shot of Jager. Raven followed suit.

"'To the night,' I said. We tapped glasses.

"'The night,' she agreed and looked into my eyes. I knew good ecstasy. I knew what was coming. The anticipation of rolling, rolling with Raven, was rising through me. I shivered like a cold, wet puppy. I tipped my glass and felt the ice-cold liquor slide down my throat with a chilling heat. A vision flashed in my head of the Jagerbomb swirling—taurine, caffeine, and alcohol mixing with much wilder chemicals. A warty witch cackling and stirring her spoon in my cauldron of a belly."

## 13

Eben paused and looked over at me.

"Have you ever taken MDMA, Mr. Preacher?" he asked me.

It took me a moment to realize that he was addressing me. I was so completely immersed in his tale that echoes of the music at Straylight were ringing in my ears. I could see Raven's eyes flashing at me from a level of awareness just beneath consciousness. I could feel *the cream* as though it were a living organism: some symbiont or parasite, making its way at will throughout my body.

"Y–Yes," I finally answered. "Only a few times. Back in the eighties I had a girl, Gina. Her spot was the Stark Club. Ex hadn't been scheduled as a controlled substance yet. The club scene in Dallas was one of the first places in the country where ecstasy popped up, mainly because there were a lot of people from New York and California hanging out at the Stark. I never was heavy into drugs, but Gina acted so freaky on it I had to see what was doing that to her. It was…too crazy for me. All drugs are, but as far as hallucinogens go, acid is the only other one I tried…LSD. Once was enough for that shit. It was too crazy… too nuts."

"Exactly. I was sitting there at Straylight's back bar with Raven, thinking *I'm fucking nuts.* Nothing kicks off hallucinations worse than drugs that *by Christ cause* hallucinations. Yet there I sat, anxiously awaiting the onset of that first wave—all on account of the power of pussy. Tell me, Mr. Preacher, is there anything, any force in this universe, more powerful than that of the pussy?"

"Well…" I started.

"Don't answer that." Eben cleared his throat.

"By the time we had both finished our beers, the MDMA was affecting me. I could feel my nervous system starting to crackle. My stoic face crinkled up into a smile. The music was changing form, calibrating itself with my internal rhythms. Raven was also undergoing this change, I could tell because we were becoming connected—or, rather, the connections that already existed between us were unhidden by the drugs. Though illegal in the U.S., some therapists still use MDMA in the attempt to patch up failing marriages. It is easy to understand why when you are on the stuff. The action of the drug allows folks to *see* the essence of connection. Petty arguments, even seemingly unsolvable, 'irreconcilable' conflicts become irrelevant to the mind that is opened to a perspective that is impossible in a sober state. Without intellectualizing it, you understand on a physical level that this other person before you, whom you had loved, is part of you in a very real, very warm and pleasurable way.

"'Come with me,' Raven said, taking my hand. She led me to another door. I self-consciously looked back over my shoulder as we neared and I noticed that it was hung with a '**No Entry**' sign. We went through and into a smaller room that was scattered about with stacks of boxes covered in plastic.

Multicolored wiring spilled from the boxes and strewed the floor. Here and there, strips of dead LEDs lay curled in upon themselves like dormant snakes. Toward the back of the room, behind one of the larger stacks, sat a huge leather couch beside a lava lamp inexplicably plugged-in and turned on. Before we even sat down, I reached my hands out and touched Raven's shoulders. I rubbed them and she made a quiet moan of pleasure. As every second passed I could feel myself becoming more physical, more primal.

"She turned and put her hands on my hips, reached up and traced my ribs with a finger. I watched her eyes as they began to swirl like some organic pair of ocean-colored pinwheels. She angled her head up and bit my upper lip so hard I could taste blood, and when she pulled away I could see the sanguine stain on her teeth. She pushed me down onto the leather, standing above me, forcing her knees between mine. Her eyes were bright, slow-moving whirlpools as she put her hands on herself. She placed them on her inner thighs, barely brushing her most intimate place before massaging her way up to her flat belly—moving up and down, up and down, until they found her breasts. She wasn't putting on a show for me, or at least not only that. She was finding pleasure in herself. I sensed that had she been alone in that moment, she would have pinched and rubbed her nipples hardening underneath her top and bra no differently. After a while, she looked down at me and smiled in a way like I imagine a feline in heat would smile, if it could.

"'Hang on a sec',' she said. Every one of my hairs was standing on end. She reached into her pocket and withdrew the napkin that George had passed her at the bar. She unfolded the note, looked at it, and dropped it onto the couch next to me. I glanced down and saw that aside from the Bud Light branding, there was nothing on the napkin but a number printed in blue Marks-A-Lot: 17. Raven reached down into her leather boot and came up with a plastic baggie. My eyes widened as she opened it to reveal a large number of ecstasy capsules exactly like the ones we had eaten.

"I watched her as she pulled out a smaller, empty baggie and counted capsules into it—'17' I thought to myself. It was about half of what she had in all.

"'I thought you only had three,' I said to her, not being able to stop myself from reaching up and placing my palm high up on her left inner-thigh.

"'It *is* only three,' she put the new baggie in her back pocket, and the remainder she replaced in her boot. As she bent down to do so, she took my hand still on her thigh and slowly pulled it up against the soft place between her legs. She wiggled just enough so that I could feel her texture. She spun abruptly away.

"'Don't go anywhere,' she said, disappearing around the stack of boxes. She idly reached out and caressed a tilted machine part as she went out of view.

"Oh, my mind, Mr. Preacher! The reason that taking ecstasy is called 'rolling' is that the sensations *roll* over you— beginning in a lull, and then building into a crescendo that can feel like the height of orgasm prolonged beyond human possibility, and then into even further reaches of humane bliss. I began to lose track of time. As the drug insinuated its way into my most intimate interstices and twisted them into ineffable knots of pleasure, I could feel both my vision and my consciousness becoming dissolute; I could feel my thoughts pinging about as if they were random messages generated to test the pathways of some newly created virtual network. Holding on for dear sanity, I squirmed, and my fingers gripped at the slick leather of the couch.

"The music was inexorable. The bass hits pounded through the walls, measuring cupsful of added intensity through my boiling bloodstream. I envisioned feet thumping the hardened plastic of the dance floor. I was losing focus. I could sense it slipping away. My eyeballs jumped and skittered in their sockets, and worms of fear played in the waters of the oceanic tides of pleasure that crashed in unstoppable waves upon my rocks and shores. Worms of fear and doubt crawled along my bones and muscles as full awareness of what I had gotten myself into crashed home.

"*Oh God, I'm going to start…*'

"I knew what crackled just outside of my field of vision.

"*Oh God—*' I leaned and puked behind the couch. Somehow I still had the wherewithal to eat an Altoids in anticipation of kissing Raven. The music *thump–thump–thumped* its way into patterns along my mental framework. The storeroom was dark aside from the shifting, red glow of the lava lamp burbling its bubbles on the floor next to the couch. The music seemed to grow louder and more insistent as yet another wave of unavoidable chemical pleasure began its slow build from the roots of my dendrites and axons. The thumps ticked time like quicker seconds. The floors and walls vibrated with the rhythm; my body vibrated with it. My perma-smile was like a small creature attached to my face, my muscles stretched to their fullest extent.

"If I may, Preacher, it occurred to me—have you ever considered the difference between feelings and pleasures produced by chemicals and those felt naturally? I've heard the extremes reached by means of using drugs called 'fake,' and I understand the sentiment, but I think the term is used only for lack of a better one. No, there is nothing 'fake' about the effects of any drug. In the middle of the high, one is liable to be heard saying that he has never felt more alive, intense, comfortable, or free depending on the nature of the drug. So why do some folks, even folks experienced with drugs, call the feelings 'fake?'

"Do you know the answer to the riddle, Mr. Preacher?"

Again, Eben's story had so entranced me that it was shocking to realize that he had asked me a question that required an answer. Arab Muslims say that the verses of the Koran, when recited aloud in the original Arabic, come alive in the air and shine like fire in the minds of those who hear and comprehend. It was like that for me, sitting at that steel jailhouse table with Eben Thomas. I remember every turn of phrase, every specific detail—as if the words had been branded into the soft flesh of my brain as he spoke them. I envisioned his story exactly. In fact, I can expand upon it without embellishment. He may have said, "a shadowy balcony," but in hearing those words I saw the color of the flaky paint crumbling at a touch upon the iron railing. I heard the crackle of the wicker rocking chair. I smelled the staleness of an old cigarette as it lay in the translucent, brown, glass ashtray resting on the rough concrete floor beside the chair. I had no thought of memorization at the time. It seemed as though what he was telling me was something incredibly familiar. I won't attempt to explain that.

To say that a direct question from him in the midst of his story was a dissonance would be technically true, but in the same way that a composer might use dissonance to emphasize opposing harmonies. I cleared my throat and thought about the question. I used my pedantic voice and style, knowing that Eben was one who could appreciate it. I may have taken it a bit far, but I was reveling. It was a subject I knew a little about.

"Well," I said, "I've never been a fan of drug use for many reasons, though I've sampled a majority of the different types over the years—ah, the answer comes only by looking through sober eyes. As humans, we have a certain set spectrum of emotions. They vary by individual, of course, as do all traits, but, aside from the extremely abnormal cases, we can guess what circumstances will produce which emotional responses accurately enough. Over time, a man will feel a certain way when certain things happen to him, or he thinks of such and such things, and he comes to rely on this pattern of emotional response. Emotion often being a person's prime motivator, a reliable pattern of responses gives him a sense of stability in his life.

"When a man makes love to his woman, he is flooded with physical and emotional *feelings* in a particular way. The intensity of his feelings may vary, but their character remains essentially the same, one day to the next, one month to the next, one year to the next. He may eventually tire of a particular woman, or he may give up carnal pleasure entirely, but these are variances in shade, not color. This being true, a man may sit at his desk or lie on his bed and, if he begins to think of his woman, the shape of her breasts, his lips on her nipples, the feel of her soft skin beneath his questing fingers, her sounds of pleasure and love, then each time he considers such things, there will be an accordance in him, physically and emotionally. In other words, his memories do not contain his emotions—they *produce* them. The pleasures are not remembered, they are felt again.

"But what of the pleasures of drugs? I can remember taking ecstasy, too. While on it, nothing can compare. The intensity of feelings is so far beyond the range of normal that it would be futile to try to convey the reality of it to a person who hasn't experienced it for themselves. And therein lies the problem. One of that particular drug's effects is to produce a feeling of connection or communion with others. This effect is shockingly pleasurable and enlightening while it lasts. You alluded to this effect when you mentioned MDMA as it is used in couple's therapy. While under the spell of the drug, a person cannot help but feel that his life has changed, and regret that he has missed so much in light of his newfound connection. His mind is opened in much the same way as it was during sex, but there the similarities end.

"As I said before, when this man awakens the next day and sits with his morning coffee, he may think of his former night of lovemaking and his memories will be possessed by that extra layer of physical and emotional accord. His experience on ecstasy? The memories themselves may be muddied by the action of the drug, but even if his memories were left intact, how does he recall the night? At first, he may consider it a learning experience—which is technically true. But, as he returns to the mundane habits of his life, the recollections of his strange and wonderful ordeal will begin to betray him. Intellectually, he will recall a stark sense of connection and a sensual pleasure far beyond any imaginable sex. As he considers the memory though, it seems—hollow. When he daydreams of sex, his pulse quickens, and his nerves come alive. He feels a stirring. His cock may stiffen. If he thinks of a fistfight he's participated in, his blood pressure goes up, and he mimics a defensive stance he may have used. The mouth waters at the memory of a delectable meal. Sharp experiences, sharp memories. But the drug? MDMA? One of the sharpest experiences possible? The memory of it is dead. It may as well have happened to someone else. This effect produces discord in his mind. Part of him is sure he has learned some momentous truth that will change and save his life, while a different, more intimate part of him, a part that he relies on without thought, is completely silent on the subject. Or if anything, it may say to him, 'If you want to feel that way again, do more ecstasy.'"

Eben's eyes looked out of focus; he seemed to be staring out over a vast, faraway horizon. I got the odd impression that he hadn't been listening to me.

"I had a thought," he said. "Don't be offended by this question, but ah…would you ever consider fucking a lion, or a tiger, Mr. Preacher? Lioness or tigress, I guess. I'm not talking about fucking a male."

The question took me so off guard that I stared at the man for a moment, not comprehending. Then I broke out laughing so hard that it hurt my chest and throat. While laughing, I looked around and saw a few heads pop up from underneath covers. Once I settled down I saw that Eben wore a small smile, though his eyes were still distracted.

"Really, though," Eben went on, "don't you think that the disgusting reprehensibility of the bestial act would be subsumed in a man's mind by sheer joy at such a level of conquest? I wonder if man and big cat are even compatible. How big *are* lion dicks anyway? I'm sure some animal trainer or circus conductor has tried it using a tranquilizer, or..." his eyes lit and became focused, "Some Svengali bushman has tried it, I'm certain."

He turned his gaze onto me, and I was reminded of how *strong the cream* was with him. I could feel gooseflesh rising on my arms as if I were in the presence of a late nineteenth century Tesla device, electricity buzzing and crackling.

"Most men would never have sex with a she-lion, but we don't think twice about our relations with a woman. A woman can be more deadly, cunning, and capricious than any predator in the wild. They are hardwired to manipulate us; they lead us by the nose, using our lust for them to back us into corners of their choosing. Being physically weaker forced them to evolve more subtle weapons in the battle for sexual primacy. They set elaborate traps for us, and we fall into them willingly—even when we know they are there and what they are for. It's our part in the reproductive dance to do so. That reproductive imperative forces us into the maze.

"Yes, the ecstasy had me in its grip. And it was far stronger than I expected it to be. I had lost all but the vaguest sense of time. Looking back, it seems as though Raven *should* have been back to join me on the couch in moments. Though time was disjointed for me, I know she must have been gone for at least half an hour. By the time she rounded the stack of boxes, my mind was in full tilt. When I looked up at her as she approached, the red of the lava lamp bathed her in artificial warmth. Her pale eyes glowed out at me with an orange radiance. Her pupils were pinpoints despite the darkness; her irises were huge like two moons hung in a milky-white sky

"I stared. She came to stand over me. Without a word she reached and pulled her top over her head and threw it down in the same motion. She reached behind her back and unclipped her bra...

*The police don't have to be here, I said. The man in blue stepped off into the ether. It took me maybe a second to realize the cop had never been there. It was a short-burst glitch in my brain- a tiny lightbulb blowing out.*

. . . pulling it off to expose her full breasts. Even through the schizophrenic yawings, her sexuality struck deep in my mind. This was no innocent girl, but a woman in full bloom. Anticipation warred with trepidation as I watched her kneel between my knees and push my body back into the cushions. I reached my hand over to touch one of her breasts but she slapped it away. She unbuttoned my pants, pulled them off, and slung them aside. Before my awareness could catch up to my senses, she had me in her mouth. Her dark hair spilled over my naked thighs, the softness of it tickled me into near convulsions. I could feel every detail of her lips and tongue on me in a way I could not have felt had I not been on the drug. I reached out to move her hair out of her way, and in so doing rubbed my fingers into her scalp. As I caressed the top of her head, expecting smoothness, my forefinger was stopped and poked by a sharpness there. There was a protuberance on her scalp!

"I cringed, yanking my cock out of her mouth with a curse.

"'What *the fuck*!? ' I exclaimed.

"'What? Did I bite you?'

"I stared wildly at her skull where I felt the sharpness. She hadn't moved—still holding me in her arms. I saw nothing. I felt along her scalp again, at the place where the protuberance had been. Nothing. It was smooth—a plain and regular skull. "'Eben? Something wrong?' she asked.

I was bewildered, but I just shook my head and relaxed. She looked at me askance for a moment before continuing on me. I dropped my guard and gave myself to the bliss of the moment. I felt my consciousness spin without gravity through a hidden portal and along a kaleidoscopic wormhole. I noticed, almost at a distance, when Raven rose to remove her jeans and panties and heels before sitting astraddle and swallowing me into her womanhood. Her soft moans and hot breaths upon my neck and face echoed along my pathways, and the physicality of the act became something more, something other, something of colors and numbers. I became aware that her moans were getting louder. Her downward plunges onto me were harder and more insistent.

"'Oh damn, Oh damn!' she panted.

"As she began to thrash like an animal, something changed. Raven let out one last groan of pleasure that shook from deep within her body, but it came out too loud. It took a moment or two for us both to realize that the music had stopped. It had been replaced by the sound of voices. It was the voices of the club goers yelling and screaming, muffled and quieted by the walls.

"The shock of such a turn of events brought my mind and perceptions back to the here and now, which in turn caused me to notice that this unbelievably beautiful woman was on top of me—that I was inside her. She had frozen to listen to the voices, but after a few seconds she swiveled her body to look in the direction of the storeroom door. The small movement was too much for me.

"'Oh God,' I moaned, and she turned back to face me as I said it. I shook and screamed uncontrollably. I could feel myself gushing into Raven's heat. Her body reacted to mine and I could feel her grip as she was overtaken as well.

"I looked past Raven and by some overflowing boxes stood the figure of George the bartender with his feet wide and his hands extended. His eyes, his nostrils, and his mouth were in the shape of perfect O's. The sound of screaming was louder now that the door was open. I registered the distinct and ominous smell of smoke; the acrid scent of burning plastic.

"'The fucking building is on fire!' George exclaimed. 'What the fuck are you doing?! C'mon, let's get out of here now!'

"He ran over to the couch and grabbed our hands, pulling us to our feet and towards the door. Naked, rolling, and dripping sweat and bodily fluids, Raven and I burst from the dark storeroom into a whirling inferno."

## 14.

"The first thing that hit me was the heat. It singed every inch of me. The next was the smoke—it was everywhere. Eye level was a foggy, reddish haze. I instinctively hunkered to get down to the breathable air. The ecstasy pumping through my veins amplified everything to a fever pitch.

"Across the common area from where we crouched, I could see that the bar area, with its rows of combustible liquor, was a rushing ball of flames. I felt as though I was looking into the gates of Hell. The walls all around us were burning as well. Creepers of fire crawled from floor to ceiling in sinuous lines. I grabbed for Raven's hand to make sure she hadn't gotten lost.

"'How do we get out of here!?' I screamed at George, who was staring around us in bewilderment. The yells and screams of the other folks had stopped, replaced by the rushing sound of flames; interspersed with the ominous *thunks* of falling debris.

"'The fire exit's over there!' he pointed to the right of the bar. I could make out the door through the haze, but only because it was encircled at its edges by gushing flames.

"'We're going to fucking die!' Raven screamed.

"'Shut up,' I said. "Just follow me.'

"'I grasped her hand and took the only course left to us: the narrow hallway that led back to the main club area. Outside somewhere, I could hear the faint call of sirens. We had to pass a heavy curtain to enter the passageway. The electricity had gone out, and behind the curtain in the hallway was pitch-black. A roll hit me as we stood for a moment, dumb in the utter dark. Sweat poured out from me; I could feel it running in in rivers down my back. The smoke choked my breath and it was somehow worse in the blackness.

"'Eben,' said George, almost in a whisper. 'I think the front's on fire too! What're we gonna do?' I wanted to laugh like a maniac at how I'd been thrust into the position of leading us out of the burning club—especially considering that I was naked and rolling balls—but I tried to keep composure.

"'We'll be okay,' I said. 'Just stick close to me.' I didn't know if we'd be able to get out, I didn't want to think about it. I did know that if Raven, or George, or both of them had a panic attack, I would never get them out. So I pretended to know what I was doing. As my eyes adjusted to the near complete darkness, I could see a faint glow at the other end of the hall. I led our trio over to it, and found that the light was from flames on the other side of the doorway leading to Straylight's—or to the husk that was formerly Straylight's main floor. As we stood before it, a sharp crack sounded from the other side. I would have bet that it was a ceiling beam breaking and falling to the floor. George reached past me to push open the heavy door.

"'Hang on!' I yelled, remembering the fire lessons from my school days. I reached my hands out gingerly to the door, which was of a heavy, thick, and solid wood. Before my fingers could touch it, I could feel the powerful heat radiating out. The fire was hot, and it was close.

"'We can't go through—' I started.

"'There's gotta be a way!' George yelled. From the look of him he was drunk, or had taken some of the Molly himself. Whatever it was, fear animated his body as he pushed past me and slammed the door open against an obstruction that was blocking it from the other side. It opened out a few feet, which was enough for me to see that the ceiling and the walls directly before the door were ablaze. The stifling heat forced us all backward. I put Raven behind me, but George stepped forward with a wild look in his eyes as if he had come completely unhinged.

"'There's a way through! You see it!?' he yelled, 'you see it!?'

"'George, no!' I snapped in desperation. I could not stop him. I grabbed his arm, but he broke my grip and ran through the partly opened door directly into the blaze. I knew his mind had snapped when he became immolated and I could hear him roughly laughing instead of screaming—as if fate had played a hilarious jest upon him there at the end.

"I spent no time in remorse for George, thinking wholly on survival. He had gone looking for me and Raven instead of leaving Straylight immediately—he saved us both from a horrible fate. But he paid for his good deed with his life. Maybe that's why he laughed, I don't know. I steeled myself before reaching out to take hold of the stainless handle of the door. The heat was excruciating, I knew it was damaging me, but I pulled it shut with a slam and released the handle, blowing on the blistering flesh of my palm and fingers. Raven tried to grab my hand, but I snatched it away from her.

"'Are you alright?' she asked.

"'I'm dandy.'

"If anything, the passage looked darker now. The electric lines powering the LEDs had long since been severed. Wires, circuit boxes, and disconnects burnt to melted plastic and sooty metal in the conflagration. We were shadows to each other, black on black. I reached for her with my good hand and drew her to the middle of the hall. I sat her down and went back over to the curtain that we entered through from the back bar. I moved it to the side saw what I feared: no exit. No way out. The fire had grown worse since we had come out of there. I turned back and felt along the low ceiling hoping for a hatchway, or a way to break through, but there was nothing. The only things I did find were three emergency fire sprinklers—all dry as a bone. I silently cursed the bastard who was responsible for making sure the damn things worked. Choking and stifled, I finally gave up my efforts and sat next to Raven on the floor.

"'We are going to die, aren't we?' she said. I couldn't see her face, but by the tone of her voice I could imagine that her eyes were looking far away—remembering her childhood, perhaps. Looking inwardly.

"'I don't know,' I said. 'I don't know what else to do. I don't think there's anything else we *can* do.' I slapped my hand on the floor in anger before I remembered that it was burned. I cursed at the pain.

"'I'm afraid,' she whispered. Her voice caught and she leaned over to place her body into my hollow. 'I'm so afraid.'

"She was wet with sweat, slick with it. Her scent filled me and the MDMA intensified my senses. I could pick up her perfume beneath the acrid, pungent smell of ash and smoke. Laced through that was the sharp musk of her fear. I held her in one arm as she choked out a sob.

"'Eben…do you think there's…do we have souls? Will we…go on? When we d-die?'

"'My instincts told me I should comfort the girl—tell her what she wanted to hear. Sugar plums and roses and Jesus and her dead momma. But it seemed that I was dying here in this hallway, maybe horribly. I didn't want to go out as a hypocrite. So I compromised with myself and half-stole a Hemingway line: "'I don't know,' I said, 'but it's pretty to think so.'

"Instead of hypocritical, I felt pretentious, which was probably worse under the circumstances. I wonder how often old Ernest thought about that line before cracking open another bottle? Her lips probed for my neck. She kissed me, and I could feel the wetness of her tears on my cheek.

"'Make love to me,' she whispered in my ear. 'Please, Eben.'

"Gently, aware that these could be the last moments of my life, I caressed Raven's soft flesh as if she were my virgin bride, and this dirty floor was our wedding couch. We abandoned ourselves to each other in that complete darkness. I felt an intensity of passion that I had never known. I was in desperate awe. I savored sweet memories of my past, making final peace with myself. I was ready to die. All the weight of my life lifted from my shoulders. My hallucinations came on and her shadowy form exploded with a glimmering aura.

"As we made love, I noticed the light in the hallway increase, as well as the heat. I glanced over and saw that the curtain in the back had finally caught. Now I could see the object of my passion. She was covered with soot, as was I. I don't remember feeling any fear at that moment. I clutched her desperately. Raven, I knew, was just attempting to lose herself in the moment. Through intense pleasure, perhaps she could convince herself that she wasn't about to suffer a horrible death by fire. I could see the logic of that, so I applied myself to the task at hand.

"Smoke, thick and opaque, penetrated into the hallway. I lay myself low on top of Raven so as to avoid breathing the noxious fumes of the smoke of plastics and fabrics. As the time grew closer, part of my mind was visualizing the horror of a burning death. I had read somewhere on the Internet that when the flesh burns, the nerves die– that the terrible pain of burning comes during recovery, not at the moment of the injury.

"'Oh, Eben!' Raven was having an orgasm and she was grinding against me, forcing me as deep in her as I could go. *Would the smoke inhalation knock me out before the heat boils my organs? How does one die from fire? Is it the brain that boils? Do the lungs get seared and stop taking oxygen? Will the heart burst from the stress?* These were the thoughts that found purchase in my mind while Raven squirmed underneath me like a wild animal. The sheer pitch of her frenzy swept me up with it. I looked down at her face and saw her eyes open, revealing neon-bright whirlpools of color in place of her irises. An intense orgasm that was as much pain as it was pleasure built inside me and then released into her. More memories cascaded through my consciousness: my mother smiling at me and pinching my nose, a girlfriend slapping me in the face, hallucinations and the feel of Roxi creeping through my system in the early morning. Still high and full of inexplicable pleasure, I lay silently next to a woman I hardly knew. I coughed with the smoke. Eyes closed, with my uninjured hand on one of Raven's breasts, I could feel the heat drawing closer and closer.

"One of the greatest things imaginable happened to me then, Preacher. The heat was oppressive, stifling. Sweat gushed out from my reddened skin. All hope of survival was gone from me. I even said a prayer, can you believe that? At the Two-Four they call them 'foxhole prayers,' like when the cops are behind you and you are totally wasted and you say, 'Oh God, get me out of this one and I'll never drink and drive again.' Mine was pretty much pathetic. Something to the effect of, 'Well, I could use a little help at this point.' I didn't even say 'God.' I can see where some folk get their notions of divine intervention though, because not one minute after I said that prayer, and surely not five or ten minutes before I would have become a huge chunk of barbecued Eben Thomas, I felt hot water running underneath me. It was forming little rivulets beside my legs, ass, and back.

"'Sweet Jesus!' I said.

"'What is it?'

"I got to my knees under the smoke and started screaming at the top of my lungs: 'Help us! We are in here! Hey! HEYYY!!'

"Raven got up and did likewise. She screamed loud with her singer's voice, grasping with desperate strength at this straw of possible salvation. After a few anxious minutes of screaming our voices out, a man burst through what was left of the curtain attired in firefighting regalia. He strode over, lifted Raven off of the floor, and carried her out through the way he had come. Once he was out of the way, I could see that most of the fire in the back bar area had been put out. Water seemed to be rushing in from everywhere. I wanted out of there. Picking my steps, I walked through the doorway and into what had been the back bar of Straylight. I was dazed and shocked. The molly caused me to *experience* things in such a way I never would have normally. It was much more like a dream than it was reality. My bare feet crunched along over ashes and bric-a-brac now thoroughly soaked by the firemen's blessed water.

"Before I knew what was happening, I was lying in the back of an ambulance. The sirens wailed. I could feel that it was rushing, speeding its way to the hospital. There was a mask over my mouth, and I could taste the sweetness of pure oxygen being pumped through it into my lungs. A paramedic hovered over me, jabbing an IV into my arm.

"You're gonna be okay, buddy,' he said, working his way as medical folks do. I was alive! I wanted to laugh out loud, but I was too weak to do even that. Another roll of the MDMA hit me so hard that I nearly lost consciousness. The stress must have unhinged my mind because I found myself even further gone than ex would normally take you. *I became the ambulance*; lights flashing from my forehead; sirens blaring from my nose.

My eyes were huge windshields, behind which perched crazed bird figures wearing medical garb. My arms and legs were wheels. I yawled like an injured cat—speeding along reflective streets empty of all but my vehicular self. I entered a tunnel formed out of streaking neon signs that were shaped into every conceivable form of geometry and symbology. The lights rushed by in twisting and shifting shapes. I saw light-wrought effigies of Freud and Jung and Adler and Nietzsche. I drove myself/was driven by myself into the gaping maw of a stylized Queen Elizabeth II lit in bright violets and reds.

"The vague thought passed through my mind that maybe I *was* dying as I lay there deep in shock, but I dismissed the notion as I felt that I was too firmly in place to be slipping away. I soaked in the experience. The tunnel of light symbols turned and became kaleidoscopic. Small, insignificant symbols merged and became larger, more meaningful ones. I felt as though I was reading some great and secret book, its all-important messages and instructions being branded into the flesh of my brain for later perusal. It was too much.

"All above me was light, all shadows below. Dim, frightening shapes floated about and cavorted in the dark—while the light was a pure and dazzling, inaccessible effect that hurt my eyes to view. I reached the realization that I had exceeded the speed of light; all I could see was the down-tilted face of Albert Einstein —an enormous, fat sun expanding. I drove/was driven into it, aimed at his forehead. His face *was* the sun. His eyes and mustache were sun-like features; his gaze was astounding in its depth. The great orb rotated and revealed another face on the opposite side. By the time it reached the dual-profile position, the faces pointing to my right and left, the great sphere of light had grown near enough that it filled my entire field of vision. The other face, I could see, was that of Stephen Hawking. Hawking's face turned to frontal as I sped farther on. His eye was the size of an Earth. My progress was leading me directly into the pupil of his left eye. My red and blues still flashed, but my siren had gone quiet. My entire world became a huge iris made of popping, electric light with an utterly dark pupil at its center. A great sense of awe filled me as I crossed the boundary—light disappeared, and I was swallowed into the black, undifferentiated void."

## 15

Eben stopped speaking and I felt as if I was backing away from the edge of a mountain overlook. It was as if I had been standing there, weaving back and forth in a daze, gazing at the vast scene below me, oblivious to any danger. I looked around the day room of our communal space with its two steel tables and its TV, and noticed that a few of our fellow inmates were stirring: getting up to make themselves coffee, checking for a good program on the tube. I knew Eben would not continue his story just then. He was lost in thought, perhaps remembering the beauty of Raven whom he had caused me to see and feel as if it had been myself who had made love to her in that burning building. That's something you do more in lock-up than in the free world, just think about and visualize the sheer beauty of a woman—especially when the only females you ever see are hags in frumpy jail guard get-ups, or maybe the occasional "jailhouse pretty" nurse.

Club Straylight. I never had any reason to go there, but I remember the fire and the burnt-up bartender. George.

Several months ago, now. Maybe a year. When you've been locked up, it's hard to keep track of how long ago events happened. On the news you'll hear the commentator say, "A year ago today, James Walker killed his wife Lisa with a chainsaw and threw her body parts into the Trinity River. In a bizarre twist…" and you'll be shocked, swearing to yourself that it couldn't have been more than two or three months since you'd seen the story on the news. Then again, sometimes time drags so bad you feel like you could give names to the seconds as they go by: Dastard. Sojourn. Elijah. Rick. Patel. Sex-worker. Hot Fish. Lightner. Fuckface. Tick. Tick. Tick.

The silence between us was awkward, so I gestured Eben to the chessboard.

"Do you play?" I asked him.

"Not all that well."

"Would you like to?"

He squared his body to the board in assent and pointed to the pawn he had advanced earlier.

"I suppose that is as good a move as any," he stated.

"Maybe," I said. I countered with the opening I often use for black: a defensive strategy. I found that he had a good teacher, but he played tentatively, considering every move with care. He set up well and made few mistakes in his middle game, but before long he bit on a trade-off that left him down a rook and two pawns. The game was over a few moves later. I was the better player—then again I've been playing for over thirty years. There were times during my prison terms when I would play days on end for hours at a time against old school cats working on life sentences with nothing better to do than play.

"You're good,' said Eben.

"Had a good teacher. Wanna go again?"

"Maybe in the morning, when it's quiet. I think I'll wait for chow and then read a little."

"Sounds good," I replied. I knew he wasn't referring to the chess game only, but also to the story. There would be hours after breakfast when the others would be sleeping, during which he could fill my head with his wild pictures.

Before long, the inmate workers in their plastic gloves and hairnets came wheeling around the corner with the lunch cart. Lunch in county is pretty much the same thing every day: Bologna sandwiches. Four slices of "bologna," four slices of stale bread, two squares of "cheese" that, whatever it was, would burn before it would melt. Regular bologna is soy, my diet bologna is turkey, at least that's what they say. Both are equally disgusting. On the good days we get Jell-O and fruit on the side. On the bad days we get macaroni salad made with too much mayo and relish. Only about one in five inmates, usually the homeless, can choke the mac salad down at all. I won't touch the shit.

True to his word, Eben ate and then retired to his cell. I did the same, closing the heavy sliding door behind me. I stepped over and gazed out my skinny little window, considering this white man Eben's tale. I felt an exchange occurring between us, but this was different from any I'd felt before. Usually I knew what *the cream* meant, or I was possessed of a prescient thought pattern concerning the one who would take the price. Did Eben really believe he was crazy? That his visions were meaningless? What about the prophecy the Indian told? Did he tell me about it for a hidden reason? Or was it just his way of describing Harry's insanity as well as his own? Was he telling this story to entertain me or did he want something from me? Could it be that *he* was taking the price from *me*? That would explain why it felt so abnormal—like a car salesman buying a car from another lot. Or better yet, being a man and having sex as a man does and then one day waking up as a woman and experiencing sex that way. Yeah.

Words swirled about in my skull, and I felt I was a tiny sailboat caught in a gigantic maelstrom. Words, hand gestures, facial expressions—I felt powerless and cut adrift; drawn along to some nether destination. As I think about it now, I realize that the nether place was my own damnation, my sick soul seeking its own level.

The sunlight was indirect, but I sat on my toilet seat with closed eyes and tried to absorb as much sun as I could. I emptied my mind of thoughts and practiced breathing. Five count for the diaphragm, three count for the lower chest, three count for the upper chest. Slow, measured release. In through the nose, out through the nose. Five count for the diaphragm, three count for the lower chest, three count for the upper chest. Slow, measured release. In through the nose, out through the nose. The hours passed meticulously. The other inmates crossed to and fro about the day room, just outside my cell door, like shadows of fish in a dirty aquarium. Johnny, the young white kid with self-inflicted cuts covering his arms, barely touched his food when dinner rolled around. He stared his pensive gaze into nothing. He was the perfect picture of severe depression. Eben sat next to Johnny after last chow, offered him some coffee, and spoke quietly with him for about an hour.

*The cream* engulfed Johnny and Eben during their conversation. It was clear to me that my storytelling friend was exacting the price from the kid, whether Eben understood it as such or not. Eben was intent on what he was saying, and Johnny was enraptured, choking out a forced laugh here and there. Eben's hand gestures were sharp, harsh, and distinct— reminding me of a commander on the battlefield instructing a messenger. I couldn't understand the words—they were a murmur through the safety glass of my cell window, but I caught the gist. By the end of their talk, Johnny was silent and staring inward. Eben looked at the kid for a moment before finally alighting from the table and drifting back to his cell.

The night came and went. I luxuriated in the quietness between midnight and four in the morning. Quietness is a rare commodity. Being unable to escape constant noise, hubbub, and commotion for weeks and months on end is soul-numbing torture. You always get the brazen idiots who seem to thrive in the chaos, adding to it—dancing around and playing like fucking kids. That's what they are. Emotionally stunted children.

They keep the power to the plugs for the hot pot off until six in the morning, but Eben and I made ourselves a couple of John Waynes out of shower water. We had the dayroom to ourselves, the others having all gone back to sleep.

"You know why they call the toilet paper we get in here John Wayne?" I asked in the form of a joke.

"Why's that?"

"'Cause it's rough, tough, and don't take shit off of nobody!"

Eben laughed, and I laughed with him. Of course, the truth of the matter wasn't funny at all. John Wayne toilet paper could, and often did, draw blood.

It was four-thirty, but the lights on our 'behavioral observation' floor stayed on 24/7, so time was just about meaningless. Circadian rhythms were out the window. The only way you could really tell the time of day was by the meals, television programs, med call, and court line-up. The lightness or darkness of the world outside my arrow slit of a window would not surprise me if they turned about and traded places. We sat and sipped our lukewarm coffees, Eben sharing a few of his chocolate chip cookies—a rare luxury for me. I let the cookies melt on my tongue, savoring the flavor.

"Please continue your story," I said, perhaps looking and sounding hungrier for the words than I may have wished. It didn't matter. Either Eben understood, or he didn't care.

"I awoke in a hospital bed," Eben began in his mid-ranged, but somehow sonorous, voice; his language was expressive, and he made few, if any, errors in grammar or diction. He was a true storyteller.

"There was a mask on my face pumping oxygen, and an IV in my right arm connected to a bag hung on the hook of a skinny, steel stand. There were no windows in the room, nor a clock—the walls and ceilings were brown and dingy. The only other person in the room was a man lying in the bed about six feet from mine. He was a young and smallish white man with pale hair. He seemed to be sleeping. He also wore an oxygen mask over his face and an IV in his arm. I wondered idly if he had been in the fire, as well.

"*What happened?* I thought.

"I checked my body for injuries, finding burns and blisters on my legs and feet. The palms of my hands were stiff and my right hand was blistered on the insides of the fingers. With a sick sort of glee emanating from the opioid addict inside me, I punched the red **Nurse Call** button.

"'Beeeep,' it sounded out of a mic/speaker on the rail.

"'Yes?' came a female voice. The accent was American, but the tone foreign.

"'Hi, I ah… I just woke up in here, and I don't know what's going on.' I tried to flavor my tone with a shade of panic, 'and I'm hurting. Bad.'

"'I'll be right there,' the nurse replied. As I had hoped, the pretty, American-born Korean nurse—her nametag read: 'Sun'—strode into the room a few minutes later, carrying a syringe with a plastic tip. Her nametag also read: **Parkland Hospital,** which didn't surprise me. Parkland, though it wasn't the closest hospital to Straylight, had a world class burn unit. Had several of us been injured in the fire, we would all have been carried to Parkland.

"'Mr. Thomas? My name is Sun. I am your nurse for this shift. You have sustained second and third degree burns over ten percent of your body. You may require skin grafts. You are in pain? The doctor has ordered a Dilaudid drip for you, but until the machine is set up I can give you a shot in your IV. One to ten, how bad is your pain?'

"I was still a little delirious as echoes of the MDMA continued to bounce around my nervous system. I remember thinking, *H.A.N.D.I.A—Horny Asian Nurses Do It All.* Sun was beautiful. Stunning. I found myself staring into her tilted eyes.

"'Nine,' I said.

"'This should make you feel more comfortable, Mr. Thomas.'

"She screwed the plastic syringe into a bumper on my IV. Dilaudid poured through it and into my bloodstream. She screwed in another, full of saline. The saline felt cool, almost as if I had taken a drink of water directly into my veins. It was bizarre. I hadn't fallen into the trap of needle use, though I'd been tempted enough to try it when the opportunity presented itself. Times like this showed me the naked allure of the practice, as destructive as it is.

"Dilaudid is pharmaceutical heroin, probably better than the heroin on the street, and being shot up with it by a smiling young Korean girl made me feel like I was in a souped-up opium den. I smiled up at her in adoration as the blissful warmth of the narcotic expanded outward from my spine to my fingertips.

"'Do you have any questions, Mr. Thomas?'

"'Yes, ah...' I was in a daze. 'I was with a friend. A woman.'

'Your friend is here, and she is well. Your clothing and your possessions were found undamaged, aside from smoke saturation. Your wallet, keys, and cell phone are in this drawer.'

"She opened the drawer pointing to my things, and smiling as if it were a wonderful surprise, which in fact made it one. What a beauty.

"'I believe your mother is here. Would you like to see her now?' Sun said, still smiling as if her face were her namesake.

"'My mom? Send her in.'

"Sun left and I sank back into the bed, pretending to be more out of it than I actually was. I gave the Dilaudid a bit more of my consciousness, preparing to face my mother. Mother had been a country beauty queen in her youth, still a handsome woman as she neared sixty. She was born and raised in tiny Mexia, Texas: birthplace of the infamous Anna Nicole Smith. Here in Texas, the affectations of the country *vis a vis* the city are a dusty pair of jeans next to a pair of suit pants. She left Mexia at seventeen and moved to Dallas to get away from 'those silly bumpkins,' and to 'find some adventure.' Mother is a perfectly molded example of how the outside world views Texas. Big hair, bigger boobs, self-righteous, and self-absorbed. Her big adventure was about as cliché as you can get. She landed a job as a waitress at a classy nightclub, snagged a business man in cowboy boots three times her age who had enough money to take care of her like she figured she deserved. Somehow she managed to avoid miscarrying their only child—me—sold my father's business after he died, and proceeded to spend all of her money *en route* to finding another sucker for love, sniping at Lakewood Country Club. At the time of her visit to me in the hospital she was in the middle of divorcing hubby number three.

"For all that, I still love her of course. She's my mom. I am an only child, and she an only parent. She sauntered in and a flash of concern crossed her features before she smiled, leaning down to kiss my cheek.

"'Well, this is a hell of a way to spend an evenin'!' she chuckled. 'A regular old victim of a fire! I'm glad you're all right, son. You hurtin'?'

"I lifted the mask and said, 'Yeah. A little. Gave me somethin' for it, though.'

"'You know,' she went on, 'yer great uncle Jesse Dale, my Momma's brother? 'Member him? The one that wore that old, ugly eye patch? He got sent to Huntsville back when I was little for settin' a forest fire. Burnt down three farms. Nobody died, though, thank the Lord. 'Less you count a couple a cows and some chickens.'

"I wasn't sure how to take that. I didn't feel like talking anyway, so I just stayed quiet and let my mother talk, which was something she practiced well. 'The gift of gab' runs in the family, she says. She pulled a chair close to my bed and told me all about how my soon-to-be ex step-father and his crooked lawyer were trying to pull a fast one with the money, but that she had found a crooked'er lawyer from 'out west uh Ft. Worth' and they were gonna take his sorry butt to the cleaners. Her merry voice was lulling me to sleep, but before I drifted off, she touched my shoulder.

"'You aren't lookin' too good, son.'

"'I'm in the hospital, mother.'

"'That's not what I mean, and you know it.'

"'I'll be fine, mom. I'm fine. I promise.'"

## 16

*Yet she multiplied her harlotries, remembering the days of her youth, when she played the harlot in the land of Egypt. She lusted after their paramours, whose flesh is like the flesh of donkeys and whose issue is like the issue of horses. Thus you longed for the lewdness of your youth, when the Egyptians handled your bosom because of the breasts of your youth.*

*—Ezekiel 23:19-21*

"In stories, it seems like folks know what to do to help each other—the cop solves the mystery, the hero gets the bad guy and saves the girl, the dad finds a way to stop his daughter from going down the wrong path—bad folks do bad things and good folks do good things. The answer always comes just in the nick of time. But life, at least my life, is not a story; even though it can be told like one. Lying there in that room in Parkland, I wanted so badly for my mom to do something and save me from all of the terrible things. I just wanted to be a little boy again so that she could smother me with kisses and comfort—but she couldn't, and I wasn't. No matter what she did, she could not solve my problems. Even if she were willing to sacrifice herself for me, her sacrifice would be in vain, and we both knew it.

"So, as I drifted into sleep, I lied and told my mother that I was just fine, nothing to worry about, right as rain; don't think twice. She didn't believe me—she couldn't. But what could she say? She knew as well as I that there was nothing she could do. The last thing I told her was 'I love you,' and I meant it with all my heart. I heard her say 'I love you too, son' with a painful tenderness.

"Hours later, when I awoke, I looked over and saw that her chair was empty and she had gone. The pain of my burns hit me full on, but that pain was nothing compared to the pain of the longing I felt for my mother: the one who had protected me in my innocence, but no longer from which whose presence flowed the promise of security. She had withdrawn her hand before it was meet. Anger, discomfort, and grief rolled through me, and I thrashed until I saw that the IV drip had been installed in my sleep. I jabbed my finger at the button in desperation and heard the machine whir of the Dilaudid being pumped into my arm. The chemical worked its devious magic, easing my nerves. In just moments I was away from the precipice and back to my normal, equivocal self.

"Blurry days passed in the hospital. The doctors told me that my burns were not bad enough to require skin grafts, but because of the risk of infection and severe discomfort, I was kept in-patient for three weeks. By far, the worst part of the ordeal was the bath. By the third day, my body would physically react in anxiety at the entrance of the nurse. She was as gentle as she could be, and assured me that it had to be done, but her sponge felt like the devil's burning tongue as she raked it across my burns. I could not help but yell and scream. What's more, there were other burn patients on the unit, most of whom were far worse off than me—including the tragic case of a three year old little boy who later died from his injuries. All of them got the bath every day. Their screams and moans penetrated every wall in the place. It was a nightmare. I later learned that the little boy's parents had set the fire that killed him in a drunken accident. They ran out of the house, forgetting their child until they heard his screams. It was a neighbor that ran in and brought him out. The neighbor was on the burn unit as well. He survived, but was disfigured for life. The parents are in here someplace, I think. When I think of the word *crime* I think of them. Crime is an act that is encircled by its own Hell. Anything else is just that—something else." Eben shook his head.

"I found out that Raven was on the floor, as well. Her injuries were less severe. She stayed in the hospital eight days. During that time, she often found her way into my room. On the fourth night she walked over, pushing her wheeled IV stand, and curled up in bed with me. We fooled around for a while before dragging my more extensive array of stands and machines into the bathroom for an attempt at sex that succeeded, if only just. I tried not to let on how much it hurt, but I think she got the drift because she didn't push to repeat the act for the duration. We found more simple ways to satisfy each other, once being walked-in on by a young nurse who stopped short in embarrassment, but said nothing and went about her business as if she hadn't seen Raven's hands under my sheet.

"Our relationship was too new for the conversation to be anything other than inconsequential. Though now, looking back, I wonder if there was more to her manipulations than those that come as natural to a woman as squatting to pee. She was a seductress of high order—her eyes and touch promised everything, but her words promised nothing certain. It was clear that a bond was forged during those desperate moments in the Straylight fire. But what that bond meant, how strong it was, and where it was leading, was about as clear as the waters of the Trinity River—which is to say, *far from clear.*

"I've thought about Raven quite a bit as I've tried to figure this whole thing out, since she seems to be the first link in the chain. I've played historical psychologist. She was one of those folk who seem to live by some hidden set of rules that no one else can quite pin down. As a young girl, she had learned to play enigmatic and mysterious games as a defense mechanism. As many pretty young girls do, she soon realized that being mercurial was not only a good defense, but also an effective way to go about getting what she wanted from others—especially boys and men. As she became adept at manipulation, accustomed to its use, it wended its way into the warp and woof of the weave of her persona. Who can blame her? The essential fact of her life was that she was a lonely little girl—marginalized and objectified by those closest to her. Who, without guidance, would accept such circumstances willingly? Who, without being shown another way, can accept the bitter truth of failure when a seductive lie is so readily available?

"Raven's answer to the crisis caused by her moving from girlhood into adolescence was to make herself the chiefest object of her own manipulations. She is far from alone in this. I believe there are two categories of this type of person. The first, being the best, the *professionals* at this *modus operandi*, both female and male, often become your politicians, your criminals, your lawyers, your gold digging housewives, and the like. Not to say that all of such types are governed by this—they become the impenetrable fake manipulators, barely qualifying for human. The second, the *imperfect* manipulators, such as Raven, become your alcoholics, your drug addicts, your musicians, your artists and poets, some of your walking tragedy, depressive types—forever haunted by their own conscience. And yet, lacking the will and/or desire to backtrack and find a clear pass through the woods. Unlike with the first group, the truth bubbles up from deep places and rips their worlds apart.

"Raven may have been dating a man for a few months, having convinced herself that he was a good prospect because of his stability and promise of security. She could just about make herself believe that she wasn't faking it when they made love, telling herself it was a small price to pay for the life she would get in return—forcing herself to enjoy it as much as she could; performing for him in every way. The closer she gets to him, as obligation and responsibility come into play, the more her entire life becomes a performance. Until…

"One night she gets up after doing her duty and goes into the bathroom to clean herself off and she looks in the mirror. She may explode then and there, leaving her oblivious boyfriend dumbfounded. Most likely she will go fuck the fingernails off of whatever boy she'd had her eye on lately (and there would be one, always.) Either way, once she looks in that mirror, the jig is up, the illusion is shattered. She would never be able to keep the sham going once it stared her in the face. Dissatisfaction with her life fosters another lie, and the cycle repeats. Worse, cycles form within cycles with bubbles of truth exploding everywhere—causing collateral damage in every aspect of her life. A war zone of facts and re-facts. Conflicted, she seeks out and indulges in anything that promises to assuage that hurt. She gives up on trying to plan anything, blown this way and that by the weather in her head. In the midst of the bad times, she often glimpses, but never quite grasps the nature of her essential mistake. Even if the facts are made into a diagram and shoved in her face, just like a religious believer shown contradictions and errors in their holy book, she cannot allow herself to see it.

"The first group, the remorseless manipulates, laugh and laugh at someone like Raven. They think themselves superior. They travel in uniformly superficial packs. They design grand events and show-offs so that they may properly display to each other the depth and extent of their networks of lies. The truth itself is but another tool, having no intrinsic value. They use the truth only when it is convenient, or (and this disturbs me the most) when they decide it is simply the most effective means of achieving their ends.

"These folk make Raven's life harder, make it harder for her to change, for she is half-convinced that they have the right of it, and that it is some weakness or failure on her part that she cannot perform as they do. She does not realize that this 'weakness' is the door to the hallway that leads to her longed-for exit. And that's sad."

## 17

"I had five or six regular customers for Roxi. Roxi is an opioid: an opiate that is synthesized chemically rather than derived from the opium poppy itself. As with heroin, the Roxi addict must have his fix or he will get incredibly sick with withdrawal. Addicts either become adept at not allowing that to happen, or they quit. Otherwise, the misery is just too acute.

"Before the end of my first full day at Parkland, a few of my customers had figured out where to find me. By that night, I was handing over my keys to one of them that I could trust—Rhonda, the owner of a little beer bar in Exposition Park, near Straylight. I did this so she could grab my stash and bring it up to my room. She was also good enough to see about my car for me. I'd asked her to check it out since it was parked in the back lot of her business and residence.

"Raven was lounging on the seat next to my bed when Rhonda quietly opened the door and walked in. She was followed by a man who, by his walk, his too-stylish outfit, and the fact that I knew he was a hairdresser, was obviously gay. There were introductions all around.

"'Well, we've got your car,' said Rhonda with an air of hesitancy.

"'Good,' I replied.

"'Well– there is a small problem, though.'

"*Great*, I thought, *more problems is all I need right now. Who am I kidding? My whole life is a problem.*

"'Okay. What happened?'

"'Your Honda was broken into. One of the back windows was busted out, fucking hoodlums. The stereo is gone...looks like they went through the glove box, too. Classic smash-and-grab.

"'Fuck!' I said.

"While Rhonda was speaking, Raven stood at looked at me intently.

"'My guitar!' she said. 'My baby! Oh God–'

"Raven looked over at Rhonda and the gay hairdresser and asked if there had been a guitar in the back seat, but she had to have known the answer as they shook their heads no. The guitar in the seat was most likely the reason my car was broken into in the first place.

"'Dammit!' Raven went on. 'We should have put it in the trunk.'

"'I'm sure they went through the trunk...' I said.

"'...or taken it into Straylight with us!'

"'...where it probably would have become fucking firewood.'

"Raven looked down at me with annoyed eyes and made a sound in her throat, a little growl that told me my comments were unnecessary and not appreciated in the least. As she stood there staring at me, hands on hips, in nothing but a hospital gown, IV protruding from her arm and leading to a bag of clear fluid that hung from a stainless steel stand, I saw little flashes of white electricity pop and arc all around her eyes. She sat back down on her seat with her back straight as a signpost, leaned close to my face and whispered, 'we'll talk about this later.'

"I turned to Rhonda.

"'Did you go by my house?'

"She nodded once and handed her friend a few dollars out of her purse.

"'Rob, would you go get us all some soft drinks? I saw a machine on the second floor.'

"He left and Rhonda moved over to my bed. She glanced over at the patient who shared my room, sound asleep. She then pointedly looked at Raven. The two had barely acknowledged one another's presence and said nothing to each other at that moment, either.

"Detecting some feminine B.S., I said, 'She's cool.' The hallucinations hadn't spread beyond Raven's eyes, so I was trying to keep her in my peripheral. Rhonda produced a prescription bottle and tried to hand it to me, but I shook my head.

"'My fingers are cooked meat. Open it for me.'

"She did, and I looked to make sure that it contained the right amount of the little blue pills. It checked out. I didn't want be openly mistrustful of Rhonda, so I didn't count them one by one in front of her, though I would do so later. These were Roxicodone—a rare drug. I sold it at a dollar a mg, so yeah, I kept track of every. Single. One. The hundred and twenty-two pills in that bottle were worth over $3,000 to me—money that covered my own habit and living expenses, plus overhead for the next batch of pills. I always kept at least one full bottle of sixty squirreled away in case something unforeseen occurred, and that was aside from my personal stash. Have you sold opiates before?"

I nodded in assent, thinking back to my heroin dealing days.

114

"Then you know how it is, Mr. Preacher. An opiate dealer can't run out. Not for more than a day, anyway. You may be good to your clientele and keep them happy, but if your negligence makes them sick they will resent you and eventually leave you for another dealer. There is nothing in the world that a junkie hates or fears worse than withdrawal, so most of them have plans B or C ready in case plan A (you) falls through. Fall through one to many times and plans B or C become the new plan A, and you've got to fight to get their business back.

"I slid out two of the little pills and handed them over to Rhonda, who smiled graciously, and I tapped another into my reddened palm before sitting the bottle on the bedside table, open.

"'Can you do me one more flavor?'

"'Shoot.'

"'You know Juan's Garage over off Carrol and Thirty?'

"She nodded, 'On the service road?'

"'Yeah—could you have your boyfriend drop it there? I'll call Juan and let him know what's up. He'll recognize my car, anyway.'

"'My boyfriend?' Rhonda giggled. 'You mean Rob? He's not my boyfriend. He's gay, dummy!'

"'Really?' I said.

"She gave me a look and giggled again.

"'Anything else?' she asked.

"'Everything look alright at my house?'

"'As far as I could tell, yeah.'

"'Could you go by every couple of days and check it out? Personally, I don't want sugarshorts, or anybody else, knowing where I live.'

"As I spoke, I handed Rhonda the pill that I had in my hand. She lightly caressed my finger as she took it from me. Rhonda was more than just a bar owner. The loft above her shop was a very strange place indeed. When she wasn't pouring drafts she was often whipping fat businessmen, and making them kiss her feet. She was a dominatrix: BDSM, leather, chains, and all. Curiosity got the better of me once, and led to a shocking evening alone with Rhonda in her 'Chamber of Pleasures.' I guess I got the special treatment, because the night ended with her riding me while I was tied up and blindfolded. It climaxed with her choking me and calling me 'stupid fucker, stupid animal fucker' over and over until I passed out. The memory made me even redder than I already was as she smiled and looked me right in the face, especially with Raven sitting there, not even three feet away.

"'Sure thing, Hun,' she said. 'I'll give you a holler if anything happens that you need to know about. Other than that, just try to rest and get healed up.'

"With that, she looked Raven's way for another pointed moment. Raven caught Rhonda's gaze and held it. They both smiled at the same time in the same way, and a chill that made me shiver went up my spine.

"'K,' I said.

"'Bye now. I guess Rob got lost looking for the coke machine. If he shows up here just have him call me.' With those words she left.

"I looked at Raven and saw that her eyes had grown distant. She was focused on nothing and her countenance was sorrowful. She arose stiffly, still in pain, and left my room. I didn't know what the matter was, but it couldn't be jealousy—at least not only that. *What could it be?* I depressed the button for the Dilaudid drip, like rubbing a genie's lamp. The medicine coursed in, easing my pain and soothing my worries.

"*What's wrong with her?*

"Echoes sounded in my mind as I sank into a deliberate stupor. I fantasized about Raven's beautiful body and our insane night together, still trying to put the events in order. I tried to tether myself to something stable, my sense of self and reality having been shocked by my resignation to a fiery death. I thought about the experience—the visions, the ecstasy; George, damn! The crazy fool fricasseed himself. I tried not to think about how he laughed as he ran into the flames. It was a pure, rough, mad laughter that haunts my dreams to this day. From there, I went back in my memory to Harry: my uncanny, Indian friend. I thought about my hallucinations of his head aglow while he babbled his mad prophecy. *The more difficult path was to the right, and it leads to betrayal.* I remembered the dining room of the Two-Four, and I heard Raven's sweet, somber voice and the even rhythm of...

"*Her guitar. Damn.*

"Those fucking assholes broke into my Honda and stole Raven's guitar. Since I'd thought of it, I remembered her speaking about it during one of her performances. The Taylor guitar had been her father's. He had offed himself when she was a young teenager, thirteen or fourteen. The guitar must have been her most precious possession and I had glibly made light of the fact that it was gone. *Dumbass, dumbass, dumbass.* She was undoubtedly hurt to the core and blaming herself. She had probably gone to her room, lay down in bed, and stared at the ceiling—wishing for a drink to numb the pain. Sadness rippled the calm surface of my painkiller-infused psyche.

"My musings were interrupted by the buzz of my phone vibrating on the bedside table. I glanced at the display screen. Jared. Jared was the assistant manager at Hank's: a swanky seafood joint on Mckinney Avenue in Uptown. He was a customer, a good one, though I didn't trust him as much as I did Rhonda. He made a crapload of money for a college dropout in his late twenties, but he was burning himself out fast. He was spending at least a thousand a week with me, and that was with discounts. I cancelled the call and sent him a quick text:

117

Parkland Hospital rm. 437W

Ten seconds later came his response:

**On way**

"This was how I conducted business during my stay at the hospital. My customers would call and visit me to pick up their pills. There was Jimmy the credit card and Internet scammer…hmm maybe I should try to get in touch with him… anyway, there was also Hazel, who had inherited two hundred thousand dollars from her grandfather. Grace, the stripper-slash-prostitute. Leo, the sound man at House of Blues, and Mr. Steve-o, the old, gay chickenhawk who owned a lawn service. These and a few other characters came to see me at least once during my recovery. Grace even brought me flowers, which Raven was none too happy about, though she said nothing. She would express her displeasure by 'accidentally' grinding against my burns.

"'Oh, I'm so sorry! Did that hurt you?'"

## 18

Eben stopped his narrative as we were approached by one of our fellow inmates. Limping over from his cell was a mess of a little black man in his early forties whom everyone called 'Shorty.' Anytime a man in jail stands under 5'5" or 5'6" he ends up with the nickname 'Shorty' or 'Shortdog.' If you have a distinguishing characteristic you will almost surely get named after it. If you have red skin or red hair, then you are 'Red.' If you are, or look, young, then you are 'Youngster.' The worst is picking up a nickname that makes fun of something you did, or something that happened to you. The funniest nickname I've run across is Shitstain. Shitstain walked out of his cell one morning in nothing but his boxers. He strolled over and stood right in front of the TV to watch *The Price is Right*. He had no idea why everybody behind him was laughing out loud. The long brown streak on his white boxers gave the pod a little entertainment that day, and it gave him a nickname that he couldn't shake because he was too small to try to fight forty-five dudes.

Shorty was a wreck. His hair was unkempt and flaky. A razor hadn't touched his face in weeks. He'd showered, so his odor wasn't too terrible, but he emanated a faint reek of Nighthawk and St. Ides.

"Hey, you fellas, uh...mind if I join you?" he asked, waving one of his arms.

I looked at Eben and he shrugged.

"Go ahead,' I said, gesturing to one of the seats at our table.

Before he sat down, Shorty pointed to the empty cup in his hand.

"Think I can drink one wit' ya ?"

Eben and I responded at the same time. He said, "Sure," and I said, "Naw, man." Shorty acted like he didn't hear me, and he smiled at Eben, revealing a tarnished, fake gold tooth too big for his mouth. Shorty was your classic, Dallas inner-city, street bum — alcoholic, and almost surely a crackhead. I'd been talking trash to suckers like him since I was six years old. I know and understand from experience that most of the homeless, wandering bums out there are mentally ill, and often severely so. I hope somebody goes into the hood and saves them, and music goes shooting out of everyone's buttholes. But when it comes to dealing with them personally, I have a hard time finding compassion. Maybe it would be different if I grew up in the suburbs where the homeless aren't allowed. Where I didn't have to kick them awake and yell at them to get off my porch on the way to school. I don't know.

I looked at the man with open disgust. Eben spooned a shot of coffee into Shorty's little, rubbery cup, offering me a shot as well, which I declined. Once upon a time, Dallas county issued hard plastic drinking cups, but one too many heads got busted open by them, or, more likely, one too many CO's were attacked with them. They were replaced with these flimsy rubber jobs that are almost useless. It was the same situation with ink pens. Years ago, you could have a normal, plastic writing pen. Some CO somewhere got his eyeball plucked, and now we have the 'flexpen'—a four-inch-long, bendy piece of useless garbage.

"Hey! So how you gena 'men doin' this fine mo'nin?" Shorty asked, pouring water for his coffee. He had only been in the tank a couple of days and was on alcohol detox pills. He was visibly loopy. This was just another day in the life for him. A break. He would come to jail for a few days to a week at least once every couple of months or so. To Shorty, waking up in a cell was about the same as waking up at a homeless shelter, under a bridge, in a sewer, or in an abandoned building.

"Not as well as you, but—" Eben replied. I said nothing. I just looked at the man and tried my best not to be disgusted.

"Yeah, heh! Shoo', I be e'en bettah, these folks let me ou' so'n I c'n git me a bottle that thunnahbird! Hahaha!" His laugh grated my nerves like a course file. Eben chuckled along with the bum, shaking his head.

"Them I go fin' tha' ol' white bitch stay ovah there by uh...you know where Cedar's Station at? Yeah, she stay ovah that way in one o' them buildings ovah there. I fin' that old bitch an' give 'er the bizzness! Hahaha! Ugly ol' bitch only got one teeth! Hahaha!"

I laughed at the man despite myself, and so did Eben as he took a sip of his coffee. The TV was showing the local news, sound turned down. The three of us watched it in silence for a few minutes while the screen showed the ball that sits atop Reunion Tower with its night-lit, swirling colors. The colors were a novelty, as the lights had been plain white since the tower was built. We watched until the picture moved on to a traffic report.

"Where are you from, Shorty?" said Eben.

"Shi', I usually stays ovah offa Maple ovah thah, or Market Central—o' I be's ovah in the Cliff, O.C.! Shi', ovah offa

123

Jeffahson, or by the zoo. Shoo', Nawf Dallas up by tha Lane, Pleasant Grove sometime, offa Buckner. Downtown, Sunny South, Shoo'."

"Where are you from originally, though?"

"Oh, originally? Shi', you know where Waxahachie at? I growed up dahn thah. Mah T. Jones had a haws' dahn thah 'til she passed back in uh…ninety-seven. Died o' cancer. Yeah, I went to school an' everything, growed up dahn thah—kinda ou' in tha country. You know where Waxahachie at?"

"Yeah, I know where Waxahachie…at." Eben responded, thinking. "That's just south of Dallas County, right? I35-E goes right through it?"

"Yeah."

"Oh, Waxahachie's where they have Scarborough Faire every year!" exclaimed Eben. "You ever go to it?"

"Aw, shit! Scarborra Faire? Shoo', that's where them crazy muthahfuckas be at. Man, leh me tell you 'bout *that* place. Goddam, you ain't e'en gon' believe me."

Shorty was a spectacle. He gesticulated as he spoke, with almost constant complimentary movements of his hands, head, and body. His rough voice brought to mind countless memories of my dealings with bums on the street. His voice was a finely tuned instrument. Over the years he had learned to mesmerize and plead and bully. He trained his voice and deportment to convince folks to be charitable towards him. It seems he had been just successful enough to damn himself.

"Man, it was way back in uh…ninety-two, I think it was, an' I had this black Mustang, purtiest car you evah seen, five-point-oh. Anyway, me an' mah homeboy J-Dawg was drivin' aroun' dahn thah in tha country, smokin' blunts. Shoo' man, it was some good-ass weed too, fiah! It was reggie, but it wa' like 'corn is nah. Got it from these messicans outta Oak Cliff. Shi', back then 8th Street was jumpin' like e mutha'fucka. Well, we was blowed to thah game, an' I was drivin', spinnin' out and shit

124

—high than a bitch, and I wa' lost as hell out thah on them country-ass roads. Was'n nuttin' out thah but some trees and woods, main— thass why I'z drivin' so damn crazy.

"Man this was, yeah—man it was maybe two munts after the L.A. riots and all that Rodney King shit went dahn an' J-Dawg an' me had tha' windahs dahn and we was jammin' Eazy-E 'Fuck tha Po'lice!' suckin' on blunts and screamin' that shit out thah windah, you heard me? scarin' tha' lil' birds and rabbits and shit."

Shorty was becoming more animated as his story progressed. The visualization I had of two young wannabe gangster hoodlums tearing through the countryside in a black Mustang, high on weed and hanging out the windows screaming, "Fuck the Po'lice!" was hilarious. Clearly, Eben's imagination was churning as well, for he sat there and smiled at Shorty with a bemused look in his eyes.

"...an' everything woulda' been cool man, but check this shit out. We drivin' on this road, an' it turns into this dirt road and bam! It go aroun' this lil' pond an' I'm showin' out, you know, spinnin' my tires and shit, not givin' a *fuck*, when all a sudd'n, outta nowhere main, thah's s'm weird-ass houses all aroun' us like I ain't nevah seen in mah life!"

Eben's eyes lit up like two lantern flames, and he started laughing and slapping his leg. I didn't see what was so funny about weird houses on the road, but apparently Eben caught something I hadn't.

"No!" Eben exclaimed. "What are you saying? You motherfuckers drove *into* Scarborough Faire?"

"Yeah, main! Listen..."

I understood a little now. I've never been to Scarborough Faire, but I know it's what is called a Renaissance festival. Once a year, for a few weeks or so, folks dress up in medieval and renaissance period costumes—reviving old traditions, buying and selling crafts, speaking in funny stage-

British accents, fighting each other with swords and armor, et cetera. Most of what I knew about such festivals was from the news and from a skinny kid named Jake who I used to sell mushrooms and mescaline to. He worked at Medieval Times Dinner and Tournament, and from what he said a bunch of the folks who worked at Medieval Times worked Scarborough Faire during the season.

"Shoo', man– I ditn't know what in the fuck was goin' on, man. I thought I was trippin'. Right at firs' wasn't nobody outside where's I could see, but then all a' sudden these weird-ass white folks start comin' outta thah weird-ass houses!"

Eben laughed out loud again.

"Nah, I'm not gon' lie. I'm out in the country, ain't no sto'hs, or skreet signs or nuttin, and all a' sudden up pop a bunch a' weird houses and now white folks ah' jumpin' out wearin' robes and shit. Yeah! They was dressed all weird and shit– I ain't nevah heard a' nuttin' like that. So me, bein' black, I thought, *'This the muthahfuckin' Ku Klux Klan!'*

Eben is struck with hilarity again, and I can't help but join him, the absurdity of the story took hold. Shorty laughed too, pleased at having such a receptive audience.

"Man, thi' place wah big, I'm tryin' to tell ya, an' I couln't fin' mah way ou', but I wasn't about to slow dahn. J-Dawg wah freakin' out, too, and Eazy-E was still boomin' out mah system. These white folks was jumpin' ou' in front a' mah car and shit, and I wah scurred like a muthahfucka! I told J-Dawg, 'Say, Nigga get the pistol. They tryin' to kill us!' I had this lil' .25 I kep' in mah glove box, you know wha' I'm sayin'? Man, I'm tearin' shit up tryin' to get out this muthahfucka', knockin' ovah barrels an' runnin' ovah dawgs an' everydamnthang. And then I hit this open field, man, an' you know thah wah a bunch a' muthafuckas on horses in this bitch?"

126

Nearing climax and sensing the mood of his listeners, Shorty stood, piling it on. His hand gestures became exclamatory.

"Man, horses was runnin' everywhah', fool, makin' noises and dudes was fallin' offa them hoes. I'm doin' donuts in this bitch tryin' to fin' tha' way ou'. Then, I see one a' these muthahfuckas got a axe! He comin' right at our ass! 'Shoot that muthahfuckah!' I say. J-Dawg stuck tha' pistol ou' tha' windah an' started squeezin' 'em off. Pow! Pow! Pow! Screamin' 'yeah, bitch!'" Shorty gestured like he was shooting a gun.

"Holy shit!" Eben said, "Did he hit anybody?"

"Man, let me tell ya, main. I don' know. I know I think I hit one a them damn horses wi' mah car though, 'cause I fishtailed and *Cack*! I hit somethin' solid wi' the rear fender, and that muthahfuckah said, 'EEEHOWOOOO!' But I didn' look back 'cause I seen this lil' road tha' headed through the trees, 'way from that place. So I turned an' hit that muthahfucka' at about a hunna'd, and gone."

"Oh, Jesus!" said Eben. "Did they catch you?"

"Naw, I guess nobody got my plate, thank Gawd. I jus' went home and put mah shit in my momma garage fo' a whole munt, especially after I fount out it wa' that Scarborra' Faire shit– they woulda thown mah black ass *undah* the jail fo' that. Naw, I made it, somehah, that time."

Eben sat and stared at Shorty, shaking his head. He wore a huge grin, his eyes full with imaginative amusement.

"You've got to be shitting me, Shorty," he said.

"Man, I put that on mah momma. That shit happened."

I was smiling, too. Every bum on the street has lived through shenanigans like that their whole life through, but that doesn't make them any less entertaining.

fi            fi            fi

"The intercom system crackled to life and filled the dayroom with a loud female voice that carried a distinct, ghetto drawl.

"Medication! Medication! Medication on the flo'. Get in line with ya cup and water. If ya don't have yo' water, ya won't get yo' meds!"

The amplified, singsong voice emanated from the speaker on the wall, shot out and bounced around, ricocheting off of every concrete surface, steel table, and safety glass window. I cringed as the sound waves went into the complex instrument that is my hearing mechanism, vibrating my tiny ossicles, making rigid my tympanic muscles, and traumatizing my inferior colliculus. Every hour or so, at the very least, another annoying voice comes over the system to inform us of what is about to happen next, or to tell us what to do. Occasionally, one of the guards will try to be respectful about it, but fails due to the fact that the speakers are cheap and trebly. A calm voice is better than a cat screech, like Ms. "Medication! Medication!" but it's all torturous. It adds to the cumulative effect that tries to push you over into insanity and self-loathing every day. Screaming through speakers is an effective way to produce sleep deprivation. A few days of sleep deprivation is unnoticeable; a few months of it is enough to quite literally turn a man's hair gray. "Chow time! Meds! Laundry! Rack time! Get off the windows! Shirts on in the day room! Recreation! Church!" It's an endless fucking nightmare.

After the screechy officer in the picket called nurse, someone in one of the cells yelled out, "Pills on wheels!" A few inmates dribbled out into the day room, carrying their rubber cups.

"Shorty," said Eben quietly. "Hey man, you wanna sell your detox pills for some coffee?"

"Mah pills? How much you wanna pay?"

"Oh, uh—I'll give you fifty cents a pill for the green and white capsule and the little white round one."

"Shoo—fitty cent? Naw, I'll jus' take 'em myself."

"Alright, I'll give you a dollar fifty for both. That's the best I can do though."

"You got so' sweets ovah thah?"

"Yeah, cookies, honeybuns, and candy bars."

"A'ight. I'll get 'em for ya'."

I felt a little embarrassed during this exchange. I could see Eben's desire flow around him like hot blood pumping. Clearly, drugs were this man's weakness—or one of them anyway. Seeing his raw hunger was like seeing him naked and vulnerable.

"Dry out the spot under your tongue," Eben said, "'Cause the nurse watches you take the pills. Throw 'em under there and take a sip of water. She won't look under your tongue."

"Yeah, a'ight."

I shook my head. *Disgusting.* Shorty was about as nasty an individual as lived on the planet. Who knew what diseases lurked in his moist crannies? The idea of consuming something that came out of his mouth made me want to vomit.

The nurse wheeled her cart into the sally port and up to the bean chute. Her guard escort tapped the safety glass with his heavy keys. "Meds. Get your asses up." Shorty limped up to the door and reached his ID band into the chute for the nurse to scan the barcode. She handed him a white paper cup with pills in it. He popped them into his mouth and took a sip of water. He turned away and went to his cell. The next person in line took his place. After the nurse and guard were gone, I watched Eben hook the corner into Shorty's cell and then walk back out a moment later, cupping the pills. He went into his own cell, so I stopped watching him directly, but kept his movements in my peripheral. He was rolling up a playing card, and I guessed that he was going to snort one of the pills. From a side view, his *cream* seemed to be alive and sinister. It felt as though I were camping alone at night and hearing indistinct, rustling noises in the brush not far off. It seemed possible that at any moment, the dangerous beast pent up in Eben's cell would come flying out to attack—to screech in my ears and claw at my face. Eben put the tube up to his nose, leaned down and snorted the powdered pill. It must have burned him pretty badly, because he stood and exclaimed, "Dammit!" and paced his cell, holding his face and making deep snorting noises. I shook my head as, despite this display, he leaned back down for another line—this time staying seated and making a percussive little *ahk* sound in his throat.

The drug hit him pretty quickly. He stood and stretched his arms and I saw that the ferocious glow surrounding him had simmered down to a low boil. He reclined back into his bunk in stark relief. I turned away from his cell then, sitting alone at the stainless steel table. I stared up and through the television screen playing soap operas. I idly watched a scene in which one of the rich, beautiful, villains was locked up in jail, being visited by the latest in an endless string of betrayed accomplices/jilted lovers. The wash of sensation brought up deep memories that came to me almost against my will.

## 19

*But the fearful, and unbelieving, and the abominable, and*
*murderers, and whoremongers, and sorcerers, and idolaters,*
*and all liars, shall have their part in the lake which*
*burneth with fire and brimstone: which is the second death.*

—*Revelation 21*

Vengeance is a secret lover. She is an addiction as destructive as any drug user's obsession. Eben's words about his experience at Parkland had painted an impressionist's lines of hallways, doctors, medical machines, orderlies, burn scars, and scrubs on my mind's canvas. My thoughts snapped back to the moment I woke up in that same hospital—only decades in the past, after the events of Lexi's betrayal. My young mind and body recovered quickly from the massive overdose, and the very second I could think straight the bright, hot fire of a deep and abiding anger came alive in me. At first, it often overwhelmed me to the point where I could think or feel nothing else for hours at a time. I'd never been an angry man. If anything, I could be described as an aspiring young minority trying his best to play a badly dealt hand. Never in my life had I had thoughts or emotions that were even vaguely similar to the ones I began carrying at that time.

It often started with the feeling of my fingers wrapping around Lexi's smooth swan's neck, my eyes open wide, and my arm muscles tensed and bulged as I squeezed. Violence ripped through my mind like a storm. I could see Darryl's idiotic, drugged-out face snickering at me. I could see myself with a hammer, coming down on him with it in a slow motion sequence like I'd seen in the Friday the 13th movie at the theater —my teeth bared like a wild animal. I wanted to crush his skull, to watch his blood, brains, and fluids seep from his head and soak the carpet with chunky, oily redness. My conscience was a tiny, ineffectual mouse squeaking in the back of my head: "This is wrong, this is wrong." But it may as well have been pissing on a house fire for all the good it did.

As the days passed and I was transferred to county under multiple, first-degree, drug charges, the scenes of quick violence gave way to extended fantasies of kidnapping and torture. My memories of the outside circumstances are vague and shadowy, but I do remember that I would just start laughing for what must have seemed like no reason. I felt violence in every nerve, every muscle; every bone. I felt invincible. The experience taught me the usefulness of anger—it can destroy worlds with its force.

I spoke to zero of my fellow inmates for the couple of weeks I was allowed in general population. The look in my face must have been pretty scary. I know it was, because I have since seen it on others, and steered very clear of them if I did. I ate, drank, slept, and shit—always on the verge of a violent act. It was a matter of when, and not whether, it would explode out of me; it was a matter of just how much damage I would do to the man in my way when it unleashed itself.

When it finally came out, it was bad. The unlucky one was a Hispanic kid, about eighteen or nineteen, who didn't speak a lick of English, and didn't have anyone to explain to him how things worked in the jailhouse. I hated him, just like I hated everyone else in there. He was in front of me in the line to get our lunch from out of the bean chute. When he bent over to take his tray, I heard the distinct sound of a fart come from the direction of his ass, followed by a rank smell that was all beans and Budweiser. Another time, I would have gotten pissed and cussed him out, eventually laughing it off and forgetting it. This Mexican had picked the wrong day to fart, and the wrong motherfucker to fart on.

"Say!" I said. He turned around, holding his tray. "You just shit, motherfucker?"

"Que?" said the kid.

By this time, his broken wind had reached more folks in the line, and they were holding their noses and saying, "Goddam! Man, that shit's better than dope!"

The kid tried to slip passed me, so I grabbed his tray and slammed the mushy, entrée-portion side into his face. He yelled out as onlookers and hecklers surrounded us. Fights were an everyday occurrence, and the preferred method of entertainment in the tank, but this was no fight. He yelled again, and my whole body and soul went up into a raging flame. I could see Lexi and Darryl's faces in my mind, taunting me like ghosts haunting a tormented man's nightmares. I envisioned them screwing on top of a pile of money. The Mexican kid jumped back and took a defensive stance. I was a conduit of pure, angry energy. After a punch or two my victim was on the concrete floor, and I was atop him in a frenzy. I remember the blood spattering the wall, and the feeling of something popping in my right hand as it connected with his cheekbone. Some part of me knew my hand was broken, but it didn't register as pain. I knew I was hurting this kid bad, maybe killing him, but I didn't care. Nothing mattered. Nothing could stand against the all-consuming nature of rage.

The kid was unconscious. We were both covered in his blood. The wrongness in my hand worsened as I continued to pummel him. I felt my fingers enclose his throat. I remember I could feel the strong pulse of his carotid pumping against the flesh of my palm. In my eyes, his features were feminine. His hair was long and red. This bloody pulp before me was Lexi, and she would die for what she had done. I could feel no air going into her lungs. I leant my face down to inches above hers.

"See, bitch?" I growled.

Who can say just how close to death I had taken that kid? I guess it wasn't his time to die — he must have been incredibly strong. He probably mowed lawns, or put shingles on roofs six days a week. I do know that, if left alone, I would have killed him. No question in my mind about that. Just something I have to live with. I may have ended up with a life sentence of hard time right then and there, but it wasn't to be. As I sat with knees straddling him, oblivious to all else, I felt the *crump* of a hard blow to my temple. Dazed, I was then slammed against the nearby wall. My last memory of the occasion is the vision of guards dressed in blue standing all around me, holding nightsticks and jacks. I tried to raise my hand as blows came raining down from all sides. The last thing I heard before losing consciousness was the sound of raucous laughter.

Pain.

A doctor once explained to me that folks feel pain differently from one person to the next. Some tend to be more sensitive to pain, or certain kinds of it, than others. We all have a line called the "pain threshold," which is the point at which we will act to stop any given pain. It makes sense. Pain is just the brain's interpretation of signals traveling along nervous pathways

—a defense mechanism. The body's alarm system. Some folks like chocolate ice cream, others like vanilla. Some folk are driven to distraction by the pain of a sprained wrist, others can grit their teeth and bear the setting of a fractured arm without complaint. I am of that second category, have been since I can remember. If I fell and hurt myself as a child, I would be sure to hide the fact from my Big Momma so I could keep playing. I can't imagine what a person whose pain threshold is on the low end would have gone through had they awakened in my place that day—in "the hole" in the government center.

From what I could tell at first blush, every inch of my body, inside and out, had been done violence to. I was on a thin mat on the rough concrete floor of a single cell. The only light source streamed through a square window in the door. My entire body hurt, but some places were worse than others. I just lay there with my eyes closed; trying to figure out how bad it was.

My right wrist was broken, possibly in more than one place. My right forearm, as well. There was a huge swollen ball there, near the elbow. My face was swollen, but as I reached up and felt around along my cheeks and jaw I sighed in relief. Nothing broken. My right arm from elbow to wrist was on fire. I could barely hold onto consciousness as wave after wave of the pain tried to take me under. Noticing a hitch in my breath, I focused on it and found broken ribs on my right side.

*Pain.*
*Pain.*
*Pain.*

It pumped like bloody thunder in all directions with the beating of my heart; a thousand inescapable frequencies of high-pitched whining rang in my ears. It sounded like the hearing center in my brain was allowing me to hear frequencies far above the register of a normal human. I moaned, but I knew there would be no rescue. I was in a dungeon. I might as well have been on Goree Island in the eighteenth century, beaten and broken by the slave traders, just waiting in a cell to be shipped across the sea. They didn't care. Why should they? I attacked a man like I was some vicious animal. I had my fingers tight around his throat, squeezing with everything I had.

Each throb of pain from my arm was another study in agony. It felt like someone was repeatedly stabbing into my elbow with a dull ice pick. I could still smell the kid's fart, and I could see flashes of his face—my closed fist slamming into it. The shock of fear in his eyes; my hungry anger. Time passed, and my thoughts splintered. Visions of Lexi and Darryl were interspersed with other memories—memories of the Tank Boss and being beaten even worse than this. Memories of my Big Momma holding me in her arms, letting me cry into her huge bosom as a child. Memories of bad things came like torture, like three other street boys and I cornered a stray cat and stabbed it to death when I was eight. When I was twelve and hit my neighbor Malia in the face and stomach as hard as I could because she wouldn't have sex with me after an hour of making out. How I kept myself from raping her, I don't know. I think it was more my childish pride than my respect for her. On went the procession in my head: a waking nightmare.

All I knew of time was that it passed. "Hours" and "days" had little meaning for me through the haze of the pain. I was dimly aware that someone came in and put a tray of stinking food on the floor and a cup of water near the mat. I touched neither.

I couldn't see it in the dimness, but my mind was alive with *the cream*. The tumble of memories continued, one flowing into its successor. Not long after hitting Malia, I was jumped and beaten by her older brother and his friends behind the Kwik-E-Mart. That vision melded into another fight with her brother a year later, in which I hit him in the face with a 2x4. I could see the gash on his cheek, and the blood spattered on the wall. I remembered how he touched his bleeding face with his hand, and then smearing the blood on a yellow fence, leaving a dripping, crimson handprint before he ran away.

My ribs caught fire, and I realized I was laughing. I couldn't stop. I didn't try. I had gone on over into another level of agony, something akin to shock. I laughed and laughed at my memories and visions. I remember envisioning scenes from the last book I had read before the debacle with Lexi and Max Parrot. It was 'Age of Innocence.' I knew that Edith Wharton, the author, had grown up and lived in the old money elite culture of New York City—the same culture she wrote about. I imagined Archer Newland sitting and trying to explain the ennui of the disaffected rich to my trash-talking cousin, Sadie, Who had grown up along with my other cousin in a house that had roaches and rats crawling out of every conceivable hole.

These thoughts bled into more, and then more. It must have been a fellow inmate bringing the food and water, because he came in and held my head up, tilting the water into my parched mouth. He said things to me, but I don't remember what. I do remember pissing on myself, and dragging my body over to the toilet once after a few days for a tortuous shit. Consciousness would come and go at random through my desultory mind. My laughter was becoming rawer, rougher, more sporadic.

My mind turned to when I was thirteen and my chess games with Eli. He was an old Jamaican I met in the park down from my house in West Dallas. He sat by himself at a picnic table, studying a chessboard that was set up in the progress of a game. I asked him whom he played, and there it began. "There is only one opponent" was his answer. I remembered the richness of his accent—his baritone laugh. So effortlessly would he defeat me at chess, and then say, "You don' know anyt'ing, boy."

I listened to him and I realized that though he spoke with such a thick accent, his English was perfect. He used words I didn't understand, and had never heard before. They tickled my mind as if I *should* know what they meant. I got lost in a fever dream of those days, now so long ago. Some part of me knew that I was trying to reclaim my sanity—that my mind was knitting itself back together, just as were my bones.

I met him in the park to play every day. He brought me books to read, and we would discuss them. He told me that in school, even if I learned everything they taught, I would be misled.

"A fact," he would say, "it is a lie if it serves to hide the meaning of its truth."

I didn't understand what he meant by such sayings, but they somehow rang true to me. And over time, I did learn. For example, in History I was taught about the fact of slavery, but I was never taught what it *meant*. Eli told me the reasons why so many blacks lived in the ghetto, while so many whites lived in the suburbs. He taught me about construction, real estate, wealth, corporations, and how these institutions worked in tandem to continue the status quo. He taught me the stories behind the stories that I learned in class about Colonialism and European Imperialism prior to American power, how the Americans filled the power vacuum left by the Europeans in the aftermath of World War I. His lessons on politics and economics tumbled through my head as I lay there, broken in the dark.

Eli was so different from my family and everyone else in my neighborhood that I idolized him. He gave me a new dictionary, and taught me that I should have it at hand while reading so I could look up every word I didn't know. He taught me the importance of journaling and perfecting my ability to write. He found a flickering flame of a desire to learn in me, and with care and patience, added fuel to it until it was strong enough to fan into an inferno.

*Who are you?*

Once, I asked him how he knew all these things. He was hesitant. It was a painful subject for him, but he told me that he lived with his daughter and her family. He had had to leave Jamaica in the early 1970s on account of his brother's troubles. They were a wealthy family, and had private tutors throughout their youth, as their parents were extremely serious about education and social standing. To their great satisfaction, his brother became a politician, while Eli himself, the younger of the two by three years, landed a job as editor of a widely circulated newspaper. All went well for many years, and his brother was assassinated while making a speech in the hometown of his rivals. His parents were killed as well, and the distraught Eli barely escaped with his life—bringing his wife and children here to Texas. For years he dreamt of returning to his homeland, and he would still write for magazines and newspapers there; but after his wife was killed in a robbery on the street, much of the fire left him, and he settled down for retirement in his daughter's home.

Eli was bigger than life to me, but he always downplayed himself and emphasized historical figures and the power of logic and reason. One theme that he repeated throughout our sessions pounded in my head through the pain:

"The first t'ing you should consider, when confronted with anyt'ing of importance, are the ideas of the ancient Greeks —especially Socrates, Plato, and Aristotle," he intoned. His musical accent emphasized what sounded to my ears like the wrong syllables.

"The beginning of all knowledge is the admission and acknowledgement of ignorance, for it is no'ting but a fool who says he is sure of a t'ing and cannot be wrong."

"But—but, I'm not sure what you mean," I replied. I struggled to use logic, as he had been teaching. I thought of the book he had just had me read, George Orwell's *1984*. I thought about the idea of doublethink, and how Big Brother insisted that 2+2=5. I brought it up to Eli, "I am sure that 2+2=4. I can count on my fingers, one-two-three-four. I *know* that."

"You know it, yeah? But have you not also learned that 'The whole is greater than the sum of its parts?' As an equation, this could be expressed as 4>2+2, which implies that 4≠2+2. So you see? 2+2=4 and 2+2≠4. They are contradictory, and yet they are both true depending upon perspective and understanding. Do you see? Now. What other t'ings do you *know*?"


The cell door opened, and I was able to look at the man who had been bringing my food and water. He was white and old. He looked at least eighty—a hard eighty. He had a puckered scar that ran from the corner of his mouth in an arc up to a milk-filmed eye. His good eye shone a bright blue, despite the dimness, and he fixed me with it.

"Can yeh sit up?" The old man knelt and helped me raise my body to lean against the wall. I chanced a look down at my right arm in the light spilling from the corridor. It was swollen and angry with dark brown bruises. I groaned and cupped it with my left hand, rocking it back and forth. Outside the cell I could hear the jingle of heavy keys, but I could not see the guard. The old man pushed the cup at my good hand.

"Drink, you need this," he admonished in a scratchy voice.

I thanked him and took the cup, draining it. My mouth felt like it was full of cobwebs and dust. They had busted my lips when they beat me, and now they were chapped as well. I tasted blood. When I finished the water he arose and filled it again in my sink. I took it and drank more slowly, careful not to open the cuts on my mouth any wider.

"Can yeh eat?"

"I don't think so, I'm nauseated. Maybe tomorrow."

"I'll leave the food here." He patted the tray in a strange way, his crooked finger pointed at the compartment with goopy beans in it. He paused for a second or two and looked at me, making sure I had caught the gesture. I gave him the tiniest of nods.

"A'ight then," he said, straightening to stand with an obvious effort. He made a brief show of cleaning the cell before walking out and the closing the heavy door behind him. The keys jangled as the guard placed them in the lock and turned. One of the two began to whistle tunelessly. The guard never even glanced into my cell.

I waited a few minutes, allowing the pair to finish passing out trays to the other inmates on the solitary block. I heard the *whee, whee, whee* of the wheels on the lunch cart, and the brassy *schtink, schtink* of the keys bouncing on the guard's thighs as he walked in heavy, measured steps. For most of the other cells, the door wasn't opened. Instead, the food was inserted into a lockable, rectangular slot in the door. As one of the chutes was opened a ways down the run, a man with a deep voice—a black man from the hood—yelled out, "Fuck you, Carver! Pussy ass muthafucka! I'm a' rape yo momma when I get out this bitch!" A clatter rang out as the man's tray hit the floor. The slam of the bean chute that followed was hard enough to make my arm ache from the reverberation. A few minutes later, the idiot was still screaming but the guard and the old man were gone.

Still sitting up, I reached over with my good hand and put my fingers into the beans. I immediately felt the little bump of something hidden there, and I fished it out. Whatever it was, it was wrapped in some kind of Saran wrap. I put it up to my mouth and ripped it open with my teeth, spitting the nasty taste of the beans onto the floor with the plastic. I uncovered the contents of the package, and when I got a good look I inhaled in surprise, sending lines of fire across my cracked ribs. There were

141

a few, hand-rolled cigarettes and some matches, along with a torn off piece of striker-strip from a matchbook. These things I set aside. There was  another item, and I held it between my fingers and up to the dim light. I knew what it was.

It was called a syrette: a small metallic tube with a plastic top. I'd seen these before. I turned the tube to read the label and—*oh, Christ*—it read **Morphine Sulfate - ¼ grain**. This was what was used in the field by the military. I knew that because the last time I'd seen a syrette, it was in possession of an army medic who had stolen them and was trying to dump them off for some quick cash. I was shaking by the time I got the plastic tip off of the needle with my teeth. Without a pause, I jammed the thing into the muscle of my thigh and squeezed the tube. The pain in my body was excruciating. Anticipation for the painkiller had lowered my defenses. Less than a two minutes later, ninety-five percent of the horrible tension in my body eased all at once. The morphine found the pain in my mind and body and turned it into something else—something bearable. There was still a little left in the tube, so I recapped it and wedged it underneath my mat. I did this in a deep and drowsy malaise. I hadn't slept in days, so as soon as I laid back sleep fell on me like a heavy animal licking my face.

The pain woke me. It was like an old dream. I surfaced from Morpheus' Sea into the cold atmosphere of reality. And it was *literally* cold; I was shivering. Panic wormed its way around my intestines—coalescing and finding a path to my brain. I took in a huge breath, as big as my damaged ribcage allowed, and wailed at the top of my lungs. I paused only to take a breath, and then continued with my long note of despair and frustration. After a moment or two, another inmate joined me, one of my neighbors. His rough voice sounded as though it hadn't been used in months. Within a minute it seemed as though every man on the cellblock was screaming. Even over the echoing of my own voice I could hear it. It was a dark music. It was a harmony of the worst from the worst of men. There was no baritone, no bass; no tenor. There was rage. There was madness. There was pain. This in unison was fear. Sharing one, pure, animalistic aggression. Here is hatred and the need for revenge. Here is a lie. Here the evil of a child molester, a killer.

The rhythms in my head changed, and my uncontrollable scream became another fit of maniacal laughter. The screamers joined me in that, as well. This was worse. Such a sound could never be reproduced with artifice. It could only be heard on a solitary wing in lock-up, or in a nut ward. The laughter unleashed whatever deep darknesses the screams had left unplumbed. My own laughter, released by the insanity of the pain and stress, was as nothing alongside the true sound of evil emanating from a few of the cells.

I'm pretty tough. I've always been thick-skinned. But that sound, that laughter—it shook me.

I quieted, but what I had started wasn't going to go softly and easily away. I imagined each man in his own cell, his own bleak world, laughing to spite both conscience and consciousness. Some of these men had been locked away like this for more than a year. A few would spend the rest of their lives in one of these boxes, or one like it down south. A visceral dread vibrated my nerves at the thought. Life confined in a box the size of a bathroom—a fate worse than death.

Before long, my fellow prisoners began to scream at one another through the doors. The deep voiced man did his part, yelling, "Fuck you, white boy! I'll kill yo' muthafuckin' ass!"

Pain struck up and down my arm like lightning, and I reached under my foam mat and found the syrette. About a quarter of the morphine was left inside—hopefully enough to dull the pain. This form of morphine was designed to inject into the muscle, but I knew that if I could get it directly into my bloodstream it would be more effective. I found a huge vein in my arm, the hurt arm, jabbed the needle into it and squeezed the contents inside. The drug didn't erase the pain as it had the night before, but it made it bearable.

I drifted.

"How are you to know if you are being tricked?" asked Eli. We were playing chess. I was there. I had kicked off my sandals and I could feel the soft dirt between my toes, dirt as brown as my skin. It was summer and hot, but we sat at a picnic table situated beneath the begreened branches of the giant, old oak that stood sovereign over that place since long before it was a park. There was a light breeze, and we drank sweet tea that Eli's daughter made. I remember her handsome face with its too-knowing eyes as she handed me the pitcher and the little cooler for the ice. Eli spoke to me about words, how they can be keys to help us unlock doors in our minds that hide information we already know.

"What is an argument, son?" he asked.

"Ah–well, a fight?"

"What do you mean, 'a fight?'"

"I mean…like my uncle…spent up all his money the other night on some girl he met over in Oak Cliff. He was *supposed* to save that money to help with the rent. When Big Momma found out, she said, 'Boy, what the hell wrong with you?' and he said, 'Momma, I'm a grown man,' and she said, 'Well, if that was true you wouldn't still be livin' under my roof, I know that!' And they kept yelling at each other. That's an argument."

"Ya'r right. Dat is an argument. But der are other kinds of arguments as well."

Eli was dressed in thin, white linens. Looking at him, one would guess he was sitting not with a teenager at a picnic table in West Dallas, but on a Caribbean beach with an ocean breeze billowing his clothing.

"Yes. An argument is how a person or entity goes about making others believe their point of view. It is usually a statement, or a premise, followed by at least two facts that serve to show the premise is true. Do ya' follow, boy?"

"Um—I think so. What does this have to do with tricks?" I asked.

"I'll give you an example of an argument, and we shall see if it answers ya' question. I, an old man you don't know, walk up to you and ya' friends and strike up a conversation. At some point I tell you that I know a secret about Ford cars. 'All Fords,' I say, 'run on orange juice for fuel.'

"'No, No!' ya' say, 'you are a crazy old geezer!' Now I have given you a premise, ya see? A viewpoint, but not quite an argument yet. 'But no!' I say, 'I can prove to ya what I say is true!' Now I am giving ya' reasons to believe it, these will complete my argument. Now I know ya'r all teenage boys, and ya've never owned a Ford. So I say, 'Have ya ever owned a Ford? Okay, so I will break the rules and tell you a secret. When ya' buy a Ford, now they take ya' into the office and swear ya' to secrecy. They tell ya' that they have come up with a way to make cars run a thousand miles on one pint of pulpy orange juice. They say they do not want GM, or Toyota to know about it, because it is part of a marketing scheme.'

"'It still sounds crazy to ya', but I am telling ya' with a straight face, and I am an adult—why would I lie about something like that? I tell ya' about my Ford, and how they teach ya' to go to the filling stations that are in cahoots with Ford. Their pumps pump gas into the gas tank, and then suck it back out. You and ya' friends are still skeptical until I walk ya' over to the street where my Ford is parked. I open the hood, and there I show ya' a little plastic box like the one for wiper fluid. It has the letters O and J indented in the plastic. I open the top of the box, and I show ya' about a gallon of thick orange juice. I get a cup, dip it in, and drink it down with satisfaction. Can ya' believe that, mon? I say, most of ya'r at least a little confused about it all, on the path to believing such an outrageous t'ing. I have made a successful argument.

"I have made ya' believe it, but does that make it true, boy?" Eli asked me.

"No," I said. "Cars don't run on orange juice."

"Ah, so there ya have it. With my argument I have tricked ya' into believing somet'ing that is not true. So if a politician gets up on TV, or the radio, and tries to convince the people to vote for him, what is he doing?"

"Arguing?" I said.

"Exactly," he said. "We say '*making an argument*,' ya' see the difference? It is the same when a salesman pitches his product, a preacher attempts to shepherd his flock, or sometimes when parents either try to reason with, or discipline their children."

"Discipline their children? How is that 'making an argument'?" I asked

Eli laughed.

"Boy, don't ya see? That is the kind of argument even a dog or a horse can understand: *If ya' do not obey, I will hurt ya', or if ya do, I'll give ya a treat.* This is understood without understanding the nature of arguments, or even knowing the word."

My synapses caught like a wildfire. Nothing remotely like this had been taught me in school. Already whetted by Eli, my appetence grew for such knowledge. I wanted more. More. More. More.

"Boy, we are all working together to trick each other. We help them to trick themselves, and they help us to trick ourselves. It is all knotted together like the weave of a tapestry. Remember I said that words can open doors in our minds? These are some of the words I mean. You must memorize this. Take out ya' notebook and write this down."

146

I complied and held my pencil over the page, ready.

"Write these terms:

1. Red Herring
2. Ad Hominem
3. Appeals to Emotion
4. Straw Man
5. Begs the Question
6. Either/Or

"Good. Now, above ya' list make the heading: **Basic Arguments and Fallacies.** Do ya' know the word *fallacy?* Think of the word *false,* they are much the same t'ing. These are not all of the fallacies, or ya' could say *fallacious arguments,* but if ya' know and understand these, ya' will begin to intuit the others, and ya' will be able to spot a trickster before he opens his mouth. Better yet, ya'll be able to turn his trick back on him. This will take time and experience and work, but perhaps ya' can learn—so we will begin the work now.

"**1. Red Herring**: The first fallacious argument type is the red herring. Some of the other fallacies fall under this category. A red herring is simply the act of addressing some other point than the one that is at issue. It is diversion. We all use it to a greater or lesser degree. The ones who are adept at the use of fallacy, the real tricksters, will be able to make their red herring seem as though it is in fact relevant, though it is not. Do ya' see? They use power, tricks, the ignorance of the audience, personal magnetism—all sorts of t'ings to diverge from the issue.

"Let's say that George and Karen are campaigning for class president and are in a debate before the student body. Karen unveils a point-by-point plan on how to improve communication between the students and staff, which is a major problem at ya' school. In his response, George does not address this issue at all. Instead, he reminds everyone that Karen's older sister, Stacy, had been class president two years before, and how

147

terrible a job she did. He cracks a joke about it, and gets the audience on his side. George disrespects Karen's point by ignoring it, and uses his time to connect Karen to a failure. This may have been relevant if he explained how Karen's sister might somehow affect Karen's presidency, but he does not. This is a red herring.

"When ya' watch politicians and officials squawk on the TV, on a program such as *Meet the Press*, ya' will notice that what you are listening to are often just dueling red herrings. They will rarely address one another's points directly. If they did so, it would serve to inform the audience as to the differences in their respective opinions and force them to reveal actual facts. This would not do. The truth could be taken the wrong way.

"**2. Ad hominem.** This is a type of red herring, and it can be found in arguments ranging from a marathon debate between a biology professor and a catholic priest, to a scuffle between two nine year olds on the recess yard. It is from the Latin *Argumentum ad hominem,* which means 'argument to person' or 'personal argument.' This is when a view or opinion is challenged, not upon the merits of the view itself, but by criticism of the person who holds the view.

"To illustrate, we will go back to George and Karen's debate. Karen makes the point that she and Rodney Jebbs, the popular editor of the school paper, are close friends and that they have already discussed plans on how to take the paper in a new direction. Now George is very good at debate; he makes sure to repeat the points he wishes his audience to remember— knowing that at least half of the students were only half-listening, and they wouldn't be there had they a choice. So in response to Karen's point about the paper, he once again brings up Karen's sister, Stacy:

"'Isn't it true that your sister Stacy was also editor of the Night Eagle, the year before she was president? I'm not sure we would want the paper to go in the *new direction* that Stacy would take it in.'

"The student body laughs. The inside joke here is that Stacy's name, rightly or wrongly, had become synonymous with *slut*. Stories abounded the campus about her sexual travails, in the cruel way that you teenagers have with each other. I could admonish you not to engage in that sort of behavior, but you will make your own choice. Nevertheless, my point is that George is using this opportunity to sully Karen's reputation by linking it to that of her sister. He is *attacking her personally*, which fits the definition of an *ad hominem* argument. The audience has forgotten Karen's positive ideas about the school paper as they revel in the delight of Stacy's secrets.

"3. **Appeals to Emotion.** Again, this is something all of us use in everyday speech, whether we recognize it or not. This is the case with most of these. This is another form of red herring called an *appeal to emotion*, and it is exactly what it says it is. First, what are the ultimate arguments of both George and Karen as they stand in debate before the student body?" asked Eli.

I thought about the question, and felt a rush as the answer came to me:

"That they should be president!" I said.

"Very good," Eli nodded. "Each of their arguments, their conclusions, is that they, and not their opponent, should be elected class president. Let us assume that implicit, or implied, in the argument, is the idea that they would also be a *good* class president. That they would represent the class and do good t'ings for them. In the midst of the debate, George finds a place to remind the student body of the tragic death of his good friend and fellow classmate Shawn, who had died the year before in a horrific motorcycle accident. This serves to remind the students how close of friends George and Shawn were, and causes them to feel sympathy for him right then and there. This is called *eliciting a response*. As sad as it is, the fact that George had a close friend who died has little or no bearing on whether he would be a good president. Neither does he try to make any kind of case that it would. He simply and deftly appeals to the emotions of his audience, getting their sympathy on his side. It is a beautiful tactic, for Karen would come across as cruel and callous were she to point out that George was just playing their feelings. Her only real options are to say nothing, or better yet for George, to echo the sentiments of the audience and make a show of sympathy herself.

"4. Straw Man. The next fallacious argument tool is a bit more complex, and also another type of red herring. It is called the straw man. Straw man is an excellent name—the symbol of a straw man makes the abstract idea more real and concrete. Imagine a politician at the podium holding up a doll, like a voodoo doll made of straw, made into the likeness of his opponent."

"Uncle," I said, using the name he insisted I call him, "the politicians here don't use voodoo."

"Was that a joke, boy?"

"No, I don't…"

"Save your breath for questions that make sense. Although— Ha! Ha! If ya' boil it down to its essence, the straw man *is* voodoo from the tongue of a master. Strong medicine. This fallacy is normally, though not exclusively, to be found in a speech or an editorial—somewhere that only one side of an argument's advocate has any say. The politician using it is a master trickster, a medicine man as you said. He knows his audience, and he uses their prejudices and lack of knowledge to sway their beliefs—strengthening those prejudices and affirming that lack of knowledge while he's at it. This hole goes very deep, my boy.

"Let us say that there is a state senator from North Dallas named Able Davies, and he is in a hotly contested campaign for re-election. He is in the Hyatt Regency at a fundraising event. Politicians always give speeches at these events, and in his speech Senator Davies says, 'Ladies and Gentlemen, I get up every day in Austin and go to work in the Capitol building fighting for ya'—good and decent folk, business men, church goers, tax payers—ya' people are the backbone of our fine city. If he were elected, who would my opponent Jason Wilson represent?   Mr. Wilson is a Yankee transplant. He moved here from Boston, Massachusetts of all places, and he brought a bunch of cockamamie liberal ideas down here with him. For example, he's got this hair-brained idea to muff up the way cities do business with contractors, and let me tell ya', he says a lot of big words that sound real nice. But see, he's got a bunch of lawyers that'll write a convoluted law that'll fill up enough paper to stack to the ceiling. Nobody in the world could understand it, bit in the end it'll be about two t'ings, and ya' can take this to the bank: that's raising your taxes, and regulating the heck outta small contractors 'til they can't stay in business and have to close up shop.' This is a classic straw man. The conservatives never fail to paint their opponents as 'tax and spend liberals' who will regulate all industry out of business. Likewise do the liberals paint the conservatives as lapdogs of the rich and corporations that care nothing for minorities or the lower classes. They say they are covertly, if not openly, racist, and backward on social issues. While these t'ings have elements of truth to them, they are generalizations that obscure the facts about particular individuals. They are pictures not of the men themselves, but of straw men.  Mr. Davies uses this straw man to deflect from the truth, which is that some of his biggest supporters and donors are the huge construction contractors of Texas. The last t'ing they want is someone going in and changing the laws that they have worked so hard, and spent so much time and money, to have crafted in their favor.

"This argument is very effective. It is the preferred

method of those who wish to trick the lazy folk who accept what they hear as true so long as it fits their belief system. Do ya' understand so far? I do not expect that you will remember everyt'ing that I say right now, but these are some of the most important ideas that I have to teach you."

I nodded in assent, gears churning.

"5. **Begs t'e Question.** T'e next fallacy is different from t'e red herring set. It is called *begs t'e question* or *begging t'e question*. It means t'at t'e *conclusion* of t'e argument ya' are trying to make depends upon a premise, or a point in your argument, t'at *assumes t'e conclusion is true*. Do ya' follow? T'is can also be called circular reasoning. Let me see if I can t'ink of an example ya' can understand. T'is cannot be said simply wit'out missing t'e point by being too simple:

"Let us go back to George and Karen's debate, in a place where Karen makes an argument t'at begs t'e question. Karen makes a statement t'at t'e school lunches are too fattening, and t'at t'e menu should be changed and made healt'ier. T'is is her conclusion. As evidence she brings up t'e high number of overweight students at t'e school. Do you see how it begs t'e question? T'e fact t'at t'ere are fat students does not *by itself* prove t'at the school lunch is too fattening. T'e point assumes t'at t'e conclusion is true, so it cannot be used to support t'at conclusion. If she does not bring more evidence to bear, such as a nutritionist's report and comparisons wit' other schools, she has succeeded only in calling many of her prospective voters and constituents fat. She has committed a fallacy, and if George is sharp he will point out and explain her error, being sure to emphasize how insulting she was. Doing so, he will have surely secured the overweight vote.

"Understanding t'is type of error is very important, for now you can make a filter for all of your thoughts and beliefs. Now ya' may ask yourself, 'Do I think or believe t'is t'ing based on evidence t'at assumes it is true?' It takes a lot of courage to challenge deeply held beliefs in t'is way, but if ya' do not, ya' are accepting t'at ya' beliefs may be a lie, and ya' are too much of a coward to question 'dem.

"**6. Either/Or.** T'e last one I will talk about right now is *either/or*, or *black and white*. It is simple, but sometimes hard to detect. T'is is when an argument is framed is such a way as to make it seem as if t'e question boils down to a choice between one of two t'ings (it could be t'ree or four or more t'ings, but t'e concept remains t'e same). One of t'e choices will be t'e fallacious arguer's conclusion, and t'e other choice will be absurd, impossible, or unacceptable in some ot'er way. T'e classic way of exemplifying either/or is t'is: Someone says to you: 'T'e universe cannot exist wit'out God having created it, so since t'e universe exists, God exists.' Can ya' see what two choices ya' are being given?" Eli asked, pausing.

"Let's see…," I was confused. I understood what he was getting at, sort of, but the God thing threw me off. "The universe, uh…"

"You are given two choices: *Either* God created t'e universe, *or* d'ere is no universe. Since *d'ere is no universe* is not a valid option, you have no choice but to accept t'e argument. T'e fallacy is t'at such a statement falsely ignores t'e possibility of a universe that exists wit'out having been created by God. Folk become passionate about t'is argument, which is why a simple black/white, either/or fallacy can work…"

Eli was the closest thing I had to a father. I lay there and remembered my years as his student. I felt hot tears dripping down my cheeks. Eli's voice, with its perfect words and beautiful accent, had become that of my conscience.

"Ya' have failed, boy. Ya' have failed to heed my words. Now, are ya' defeated?" it asked me.

I lay in the closed darkness of my cell and wept.

## Part 3: Good Luck, and The First Asylum Church

*Nevertheless...how do I know that I am not deceived every time that I add two and three, or count the sides of a square, or judge of things yet simpler, if anything simpler can be imagined... Possibly, God has not desired that I should be thus deceived, for He is said to be supremely good... But let us...grant that all that is here said of a God is a fable...I shall then suppose, not that God who is supremely good and the fountain of truth, but some evil genius not less powerful than deceitful, has employed his whole energies in deceiving me; I shall consider that the heavens, the earth, colors, figures, sound, and all other external things are naught but the illusions and dreams of which this genius has availed himself in order to lay traps for my credulity; I shall consider myself as having no hands, no eyes, no flesh, no blood, nor any senses, yet falsely believing myself to possess all these things...*

*[Yet even if] there is some deceiver or other, very powerful and very cunning, who ever employs his ingenuity in deceiving me, then without a doubt I exist also if he deceives me, and let him deceive me as much as he will, he can never cause me to be nothing so long as I think that I am something. So that after having reflected well and carefully examined all things, we must come to the definite conclusion that this proposition: I am, I exist, is necessarily true each time that I pronounce it, or that I mentally conceive it.*

*–Rene Descartes, Meditations on First Philosophy*

## 20

Something was wrong. Something was wrong with me. I had drifted into an uneasy sleep, thinking about those dark times in the hole—the dungeon. I awoke to monstrous nightmares I vaguely remembered. I could only recall being chased around corners, up and down stairs, through shadowy doors, and along precipitous paths. The wrongness hit me as I became aware of my body lying in my bunk. My muscles were weak and sore. My legs and feet were cramping. My shoulders and back ached deep into the bones. I felt as though my nightmare had been real, that I had been running for my life, running until I fell into a hole. There I was. I forced myself to get up and wash my face in the cell's toilet/sink combo. I looked into the streaked, stainless steel mirror, and rubbed my hand along my scruffy jawbone and cheek. I felt every one of my years as if they were weights stacked on my shoulders. I couldn't think, only move and slowly at that. I rinsed the previous day's coffee out of my cup, filled it with tepid water and drank it down. I could see darkness outside my window slit, but other than it being night, I had no idea of the time. I lowered my bones gingerly back onto the bunk, which is just a thin, fiber-stuffed plastic mat placed atop a slab of raised concrete. I curled up and sought escape.

When next I awoke, I again felt the wrongness suffused throughout my body, though it had lessened. I could remember no nightmares, but as I lay there with my eyes closed, I had an overall sense of dread. I opened my eyes and found Eben standing outside my cell with a faraway look in his eyes. Sharp spikes of color radiated from his body, and sinuous black lines writhed and undulated about the area of his belly. I had to look through all of that *cream* to see that he was gesturing to me with his cup.

"Coffee?"

I nodded assent and swung my legs off my bunk, planting my bare feet on the cold concrete. I pressed my fingers into my temples and tried to massage some of the tension away. As I came fully conscious, the feeling of existential dread simmered down to a low boil of uneasiness. I stood and hit the green button that unlocked my cell door as Eben walked up to it, carrying his hotpot full of hot water, his cup, and a four-ounce bag of instant coffee. I pushed the heavy door open along its tracks, and he stepped in. I still felt like hell as I handed him my cup and sat down on my bunk, back against the smooth wall.

"You don't look so good," Eben said.

"I'll be alright."

"Want me to come back later? Let you rest?"

"No. Really, man, I'm fine—coffee'll help," I told him. The shapes, colors, and images dancing and weaving around the man were a display too convoluted for me to look at for long. When he handed me my cup, I used it as an excuse to look away. I kept my eyes on the dark, steaming liquid. Coffee.

In a place absent almost all other stimuli, coffee reigns as the number one head change. Caffeine is the world's most used drug by far, and it's easy to see why from in here. The first sip began to rejuvenate me; and by the second or third swallow I was intent and fully conscious.

Eben remained silent for a while, sensing my mood. The toilet is on the other side of a little half-wall from my bunk, so the only two places for him to sit were on the bunk with me, or on the floor at my feet. He chose the floor, and sat down Indian-style, knees touching the concrete of my bunk and back against the wall. I was glad that he was below eye level, so that the menagerie of *Cream* seemed contained. He sipped his coffee while I gathered myself.

"Continue, please," I said with a degree of solemnity. Eben began with a rough voice that smoothed over as he continued his story from the day before:

"On the day she was discharged from the hospital, I told Raven she could stay at my place if she wanted, a proposition she accepted without hesitation. I also allowed her the use of my Honda, which was convenient for us both. I had her service my Roxi customers, and she did a little Molly business on the side. She'd only been selling the stuff for a couple of months, and wasn't really a dealer *per se*. Her supply was a stiffy named Green who tended bar at a place called First Asylum Church, located on Henderson a block or two off of lowest Greenville avenue and three blocks from my place. Green and I were acquainted, though not well, and I wasn't close enough to hate him, but I did very much dislike the arrogant prick. Here was the George connection. George and Green had been friends, and played in a band together years ago, back when Dallas had a relevant rock and roll scene. The band was called *Black & Curly* and Green was the front man. I'll admit they had talent— George was a nightmarishly badass bass player—and, as did several local bands of the era, they wound up getting signed by a major label. Epic, I think.

"At that point, Green, who was already a notorious

158

asshole, became incorrigible. He acted like he was King Shit, strutting his skinny ass all over town—loud, bombastic, and drunk. I hated it for George, but, when their record flopped, and their tour got cancelled in progress, they ended up owing the label, along with everybody else they had deals with a shitload of money that they didn't have. The icing on the cake was the night they broke up, Green got wasted during a show at Trees and got beat up on stage by one of the bouncers. They became the laughingstock of the scene for a good while. The old heads still bring it up on occasion.

"Dickheads are successful so often that it is particularly sweet to watch one of them fall from grace. I mentioned all of this to Raven, but she apparently liked Green; I suspected she had probably slept with him at some point. That made my blood burn just thinking about it. That had more to do with my feelings about him than any kind of jealousy, although looking back, I'm sure I was being a little possessive.

"She was moving a little Molly for him here and there for free doses and spending money. I told her it was her business, just not to sell to anyone new, or that she didn't know, out of my car.

"'I'm not stupid, Eben,' she said.

"'Yeah, neither are all those fools sitting in Sterret right now for selling to an undercover. Don't sell when you're drunk or high, either.'

"'Yes, boss.'

"She visited me every night at the hospital, and we worked out a routine where she would jump on top of me for a quick fuck after the nurse would do her rounds at midnight. The second night we did that, I glanced over at my roommate's bed and caught him masturbating under his covers, watching Raven grind on me. The kid hadn't spoken more than two words to me the whole time I was there, and he seemed a little slow, so I let it go. Especially since Raven hadn't noticed (I guess she

159

hadn't). Hell, what *could* I say? I probably would have been doing the same thing at his age. The kid's only visitor was his grandmother, and she was as quiet as he was. Who knows how long it had been since he had gotten laid?

"With the Dilaudid on top of my normal, daily doses of Roxi, my drug tolerance became higher than a giraffe's pussy. By the time I was released from Parkland, two weeks after Raven's release and nearly a month after the fire, I had to replace the Dilaudid with more Roxi. I tried to get the burn doctors to prescribe me the Roxi, but the best I could get out of them was Norco. I calculated it and, had I been paying my prices, my habit rose to the level of fourteen-hundred dollars a week, give or take. Resourceful as I was, this was unsustainable. I was trying to work out a solution to my problem when Raven arrived at the hospital to pick me up.

"'Hey, Cowboy, you ready to go home?' she said with a lascivious smirk. I dressed and gathered my things. When I bent to pull my jeans on, I glanced over and caught my roommate watching me. He looked away quickly—guiltily.

"'Shit,' I said.

"'What?' Raven asked, turning.

"'Nothing. I just nearly caught my dick in my zipper.'

"'Are you okay?' she asked with real concern in her voice.

"'Yeah, I caught myself before it did any damage.'

"'I'll have to kiss and make it better, just in case.'

"As we walked out the door, I looked back at the kid. He was staring. He jerked his eyes away and out the window. I chuckled.

"'Wanna go eat something?' Raven asked as we walked down the sterile hallway. I walking gingerly on my still-raw feet.

"'Do you?' I said, putting a hand on the perfect curve of her hip. We both stepped a little quicker.

"I rented a two-bedroom house built in the 1950s; it's in the old Dallas neighborhood called the M-streets. True to form, I sat at the corner of Miller and McMillan, two blocks west of Greenville Ave. and fifteen blocks, give or take, south of Mockingbird Lane. My landlords were an older couple who lived in the southern suburb of Waxahachie, and they let me do as I pleased so long as I paid the rent more or less on time, and didn't do too much damage to the place. The house was a non-descript, off-white brick, with black trim in need of paint. I half-assed kept the yard and hedges in order, but it's pretty safe to say I was never in the running for the M-streets Yard of the Month award.

After we got to my house and fulfilled our promises to each other, Raven and I lay in my bed, naked. I studied her body philosophically.

"'So', she said, 'I knew calling the cops wasn't an option, and I um...well, I happen to know a private investigator. So I called him.'

"'What the fuck are you talking about?' I asked her.

"'Oh, I thought I told you,' she replied mercurially. Is there anything a woman does while naked in bed that isn't mercurial?

"'My guitar. I can't just let it go. It was my dad's and...'

"Her eyes welled with tears and she turned to face the wall. By instinct I pulled her close, trying to give her comfort.

"'I know– I know,' I said, 'I remember you telling the story about it one night from the stage.'

"She turned her body back to me, put her face in my chest, and let her tears spill from their cups. I felt the hot wetness of them on my skin. She said nothing more, but she didn't have to. I considered that I found myself completely at the mercy of Raven's authenticity. My lust for her and my sympathy combined to make a cocktail of submissive feelings. This frightened me and I reached for a pill, but I forced my hand away from the bottle on the bedside table.

"Raven's few minutes of crying made me think of an afternoon shower. When it stopped, she wiped her eyes, arose, and walked naked into the kitchen. She returned with two fine but mismatched wine glasses. The one she handed me was almost a goblet. They were filled with a very pale white wine.

"'Pinot?' I asked.

"'Yeah– I'm a classy drunk.'

"'Where'd you get these glasses?'

"'They had a garage sale two streets over, I also got a marine's dress uniform for five dollars; it's pretty cool. It'll probably fit you.'

"I had to shake off the image of me in the marine's uniform. I took a sip of my wine. I admit that at the time I felt I was some sort of rebel aristocrat—how could I not? I had just ravished this beautiful young lady, and now the same was nakedly serving me wine in a goblet. It seemed I could just squint my eyes and be in a four-poster bed draped in crimson and gold— high ceilings above and thick woven rugs beneath, gold coins and emeralds and ivory pendants strewn about with great apathy. There came about a deep hidden sense in me that I was entitled to such a life, and now—here it is! I held the fancy for as long as I could before it fell and shattered on the hard rocks of an undeniable reality. Raven left me in my reverie to return with the half-empty bottle of chilled Pinot Gris, and refilled our glasses before I spoke.

"'So this...private dick, what did he say?'

"'He called today and said he got one of his cop buddies to check the pawn shop registries, but nothing's turned up yet. He says he wants to meet up tomorrow night.'

"'Meet up?' I asked. 'How do you know this guy, anyway?'

"'Oh, well—we dated a couple years ago. Wasn't serious.'

"'Great.'

"I reached over to my pill bottle, popped one, and washed it down with the last of the wine. So much for will power.

"'I'm guessing you bought more than one bottle,' I said, wearing a slight smile.

"She lifted her lithe form and danced out the door to fetch the wine. A man is entirely defenseless in the presence of a beautiful, sexy, naked and willing woman, but he must always act as though he is on equal footing with her, if not in possession of the upper hand. No matter how sweet she thinks she is, if a man shows a woman too much weakness at the wrong moment, she will thrash him and leave him hanging out to dry. Biology demands it of her. One way or another, she will always comply.

## 21.

"Harry had come to visit me and Raven in the hospital, bearing flowers and the well-wishes of our mutual friends and acquaintances at the Two-Four. It seems the prevailing opinion at the rumor mill was that Raven and I had gone into the club and gotten sloppy drunk, which was why we hadn't been able to get out with the other club-goers. Further, that George the bartender, known on the fringes of Two-Four society, died a horrible and avoidable death trying to save our drunk asses. According to Harry, the old heads at the Club Two-Four were nodding sagely and placing all the blame fully and squarely on me.

*"And why wouldn't they?* I thought to myself. *Raven lives there and plays music, and everyone loves her. Hardly anyone there knows or likes me, and none of them would consider me a good match for her.*

"Raven got pissy about the rumors and called some of her friends for confirmation. This went a long way towards solidifying her decision to stay at my house instead of going back, which of course fueled more rumors and stoked hot, angry jealousies.

"The second day after I left Parkland was a Thursday and that evening at ten Raven was to play and sing at the First Asylum Church which, despite the fact that Green worked there, was one of my most favorite places in the universe. 'The Church' as everyone called it, was opened on the site of a failed lower Greenville restaurant, just blocks from my house. The owner/proprietor was an ancient codger who sported little tufts of white hair over his ears, his pate being otherwise bald. His eyes were a violent and watery blue, and he pointed them around with the religious zeal of a seventeenth century puritan pastor. He went by the name of Potter Harry, and many of the bar regulars would swear it was his real name. Indeed, it was the name printed on the liquor and occupancy licenses posted on the wall behind the main bar.

With the church, what everyone thought was an advertising gimmick had become a cultural phenomenon. Potter had clearly spent half his life collecting various items from old asylums and mental hospitals. He had everything from the arcane to the aseptically modern. When he opened the bar, he adorned it with these artifacts, the quantity and quality of which made the place more a full-scale mental illness museum than a theme bar. Rumor had it that Potter himself was a psychiatrist, and had been the administrator of a state hospital somewhere up north (he did indeed have a thick Yankee accent). The darker of that brand of rumor said that he had been prosecuted and did time in Maine, Connecticut or Vermont for conducting illegal experiments on his patients. It was easy to understand the why of the rumors once you had met the man. He was the perfect picture of a mad scientist: economical, enigmatic, brilliant, and scary.

"The church was a disturbing place that was somehow comforting at the same time. All of the seating was heavily padded. The lighting was dim and private both day and night. Tight spotlights displayed the artifacts and lit framed documents depicting unusual case studies, experiments, and neurotic symptoms. You would sit at a table and find photographs and handwritten notes trapped under hard gloss for your perusal.

165

There were tasteful effigies, busts, and portraits of famed psychiatrists and psychologists: Freud, Jung, Adler. There was even a huge, leather bound, old and dusty edition of Freud's *Interpretation of Dreams* open upon a low mantle like a bible.

"The greatest aspect of the Church though, wasn't the artifacts, the ambience, or even Potter—it was the customers themselves. When it first opened, must have been five years ago now, Potter hired young men and women to go to the larger mental health facilities, public and private, and pass out flyers to both patients and staff—

**GRAND OPENING!!! FIRST ASYLUM CHURCH BAR & GRILLE, Mental Patients! Bring in your medicine bottles and you will receive 25% off! Staff at a mental health facility? Bring your credentials, 25% off your bill!**

"The effect was spectacular and overwhelming. The church became the talk of the psychiatric community, and hundreds became regulars of the place within weeks of its opening. Nearly all of the regulars were able to lay claim to the discount. Students at nearby SMU got wind of the place and began patronizing as well. The First Asylum Church was undoubtedly one of the strangest places in the world, and I felt right at home there.

"Next evening, after servicing my clientele, the time finally came for us to go to the church and meet with Raven's private eye. Raven wasn't particularly high maintenance or prissy, but she was a woman. It being Friday night, and given that she was playing a show, she took her time getting ready. I watched her dress and apply her make-up, and I noticed that she always had a full wine glass near to hand.

"'Hitting it a little early, aren't we?' I asked.

"'Yeah, well…look at this shit.' She handed me a neon flyer.

"It was from the church, and for that night. It had been crumpled into a ball and then smoothed back out. A classic photo of Freud stared out from the center surrounded by smiling images of models in bikinis, lounging this way and that. At the top was a playbill and the main event listed was: '**WET T-SHIRT CONTEST!**' at 11pm. Beneath that was Raven's name and 10pm, and beneath her was printed '**Gwen James, P.H.D.- Suicide Awareness & Prevention.**' Deciding to joke with her a little, I said, 'You've got a problem opening for the wet t-shirt contest?'

"'Wet t-shirt contest? Wet t-shirt contest?! I'll probably *be* in the fucking wet t-shirt contest! I'm fucking pissed about the fucking *professor* I'm following. Suicide awareness? Jesus *Fuck.*'

"'Well...just have fun with it,' I said. 'You can open with your Elliott Smith cover, what is it? *Going Nowhere*? I love that song! Oh, and I bet you could kill with a version of *Rape Me*. Close with that, they'll be dying for it.'

"'Fuck off,' she said. 'I mean it, fuck off.'

"Yeah. So I fucked-off.

"I loaded Raven's spare guitar (also a Taylor acoustic/electric) and amplifier (a tan-colored Fender) into my Honda and we left. Her outfit was a study in sepia. Her pants hugged her curves suggestively, as did her perfectly fitting top. The effect was sensual without being overtly sexual. She wore a large ring on her right ring finger that displayed the effigy of a cat's face with staring, pearly eyes. She had on one silvery necklace hung with a pale stone.

"Something about the effect kicked off my hallucinations. Raven became other than human as she sat there next to me in the passenger seat. I couldn't say exactly what, but there was something in her look that was vampiric. Was her skin paler? Were those fangs pooching out her lips? Perhaps. Certainly there was a look of predation in her eyes. A visceral fear crept up my spine and seized my heart as though I had suddenly found myself seated two feet away from a coiled rattlesnake. I knew that I was hallucinating, and that I was in no real danger, so I tried to be calm and drive the few blocks to the

Church.  Raven made some chatty comments, but I was too horrified to make a response. I held the wheel with a white-knuckle grip and I stared straight ahead, focused on my destination. By the time we reached the place I was covered in sweat, even though the outside temperature was near freezing. My horror subsided, but Raven still glowed with an otherworldly radiance. She had me pull up to the front on Greenville Ave. She jumped out, ran in, and returned with two burly bouncers who took her equipment out of my back seat and spirited it away.

"A sharp knock at my window startled me. I thumbed the
window button and found a man of about five feet in height. He wore the very thickest and ugliest pair of coke-bottle glasses that I had ever seen. The man had two small magnifying glasses on his face. The effect made his already diminutive eyes look tiny and distorted. He also wore an idiot grin; taken in altogether, he was a thoroughly disturbing individual.

"'Hi, Hi—Mis-s-s Rav-v-v-ven,' to top it off, he spoke with a terrible stutter that made him almost unintelligible.

"'C-c-can-n-n I-I puh-puh-puh-puh-p-park-k-k ya-ya-your c-car?' he turned to me, still grinning. I felt ashamed at myself at being disgusted by the man.

"'He's fine, let him do it,' Raven said. After a brief hesitation I decided to trust her judgment and I put my keys into his hand. As I exited the vehicle, I gave him a five-dollar bill.

"'Please be careful.'

"'I-I wuh-wuh-will.'

"As Raven and I entered the building, none other than Mr. Potter Harry himself was standing near the podium greeting his guests. His eyes lit when he saw us.

"'Ah, Raven!' he said, 'your show is going to be perfect!' He made this statement with so much confidence and aplomb that it was difficult not to be carried away by his charismatic persona. He had to be in his mid to late seventies, if not older, but he was compact and full of vigor. I had met Potter twice before, but only briefly. He certainly didn't remember my name.

Introductions were made as he pulled us beyond the foyer and into the lounge area proper. It contained the two notorious pool tables that had unbalanced balls that curved this way and that when you hit them, a few booths, and a small bar.

"At the bar, Potter said to the bartender, 'Suri–uh,' he cleared his throat and turned to us: 'Can I offer you a drink? On the house, of course.'

"'I'll have a jager bomb and a white wine, something good,' Raven said.

"'Whiskey and Dr. Pepper,' I said. Potter looked at me.

"'That sounds good, I'll have the same. Bourbon, if you'd be so kind, Suri.'

"'I don't really feel like it, Mr. Harry, but okay,' Suri said. She was a dark-skinned, foreign-looking girl—one of those who could pass as either Arabic or Hispanic. Pretty. She looked to be twenty-one, maybe twenty-two. Her backtalk was the way at First Asylum Church. Potter encouraged them to express whatever feelings they had verbally, so long as they did their jobs as well.

"'Thank you, Suri! Tell me, how did your date with Miguel go last night?' asked Potter of his bartender.

"'Well,' she spoke while pouring the wine, 'it was okay, I guess. We finally had sex, but honestly, it was nothing spectacular.'

"'And whose fault was that?' he asked her.

"'His.'

"'Really? Are you so sure?'

"'I mean, he went too fast, and he came too quick. And then he just lay back with his hands behind his head and acted like it was great.'

"'He went too fast? Did you ask him to slow down? Did you think that maybe you excited him so much that he couldn't help himself? You've been dating for two months now; he was probably in a frenzy. Next time, just tell him what to do and be firm about it! Do you hear?'

"'Yes, sir.'

"Suri handed us our drinks; I realized I was getting a hard-on and staring at the girl with my mouth open.

"'What?' she said to me.

"Raven kicked my foot, and we turned away. At that moment, Brandi walked into the lounge and joined our party. Brandi was also a musician, and often played as Raven's accompaniment. When it comes to social interactions my personality sits firmly in the 'withdrawn' category, but next to Brandi I'd be considered a positive social butterfly. With her it was a pathology—she was a textbook phlegmatic. She was small and thin, a hundred pounds with a wet coat on. She had a svelte beauty, pretty in her way; she was younger than Raven, maybe twenty-four or five. She had pale, thin hair that hung naturally straight, and large brown eyes. She stood in a closed stance, arms crossed, self-consciously darting her eyes this way and that. Early evening had arrived, and the lounge was filling with people.

"Potter offered Brandi a drink, but she declined with a half-hearted *no thanks.* Potter's eyes became even brighter with excitement as he rubbed his hands together.

"'We have a special exhibit,' he said. 'Come.'

"The three of us followed him through the back of the lounge and into the restaurant area, and then behind that into a hall that led to the exhibits—the farthest extremity of the church. We passed through a thick, velvety-green curtain. Potter held it open for us, and in a deep voice said, "Behold!"

"I walked in with a feeling of curious delight on account of Potter Harry's showmanship, which made the shock of the moment that much greater as I stepped unaware into a scene directly out of a madman's hell. My instincts kicked in while my mind reeled, and I pushed my arms back to keep the women on the other side of the curtain in an attempt to save them the shock:

"The first thing that hit me was the stench of fresh feces. Before me was a pane of safety glass that ran from floor to ceiling. It had a row of golf ball sized holes punched out near the top. Behind the glass, and on display, was a small, padded cell that was perhaps 15 x 15 feet. Crumpled up on the floor of the place lay an orange jumpsuit, and standing in the middle of the cell was a man staring directly into my eyes. As he looked at me with the severest of expressions, he held in his hands two clods of what must have been his own feces. He was applying it liberally to the skin all over his body, including his face, as if he were lotioning up for a sunbath. He was naked and hairy. His stained penis hung there in his pubis like an upside-down, deformed, featherless pigeon.

"Potter Harry stepped up beside me, staring into the cell with a truly shocked look on his face. Clearly, his plans had gone awry. Raven took one whiff and exited, but I noticed Brandi stealing a glance at the man before following her. Potter shook himself and began to move.

"'Jesus Christ!' he yelled. 'We can't let anyone see this! Especially the doctors, oh Christ!'

"The man on display tilted his head up and began to yell, 'Jesus Christ! Jesus Christ!' over and over. Potter Harry took his phone in hand and dialed a contact.

"'Who the hell do you think it is, you dumb son of a bitch? You get your ass down here now, and get your fucking patient out of here! And you'd better bring a fucking water hose!...What?... He's naked and smeared shit all over himself! You said he was fairly stable! What if he would have done this in front of the MHMR people? They would have had us both thrown in jail. Idiot! Get your ass down here.'

"Potter turned a smile on me, 'Jesus Christ! Jesus Christ!' ringing in the background.

'Eben, right? I'll give you a thousand dollars if you help me make sure no one comes through that curtain.'

"'Make it fifteen-hundred and we've got a deal,' I said, taking out a pill and chewing it up. Potter laughed.

"'Deal,' he said, and we shook.

"I asked no questions, but it was clear that the man who showed up to collect the mental patient from the church's cell was no doctor. If I had to guess, I'd say he was a family member or caregiver trying to make a quick buck under the table.

Potter's earlier display of emotion wasn't repeated. In fact, he went about his business and handled the particulars as if all were going according to plan. The caregiver, a fat, slobbish character by the name of Bud, seemed abashed and obsequiously went about getting his charge out the side service door and into his van, before going back in and removing the excrement from the floor and walls. Luckily for me, it was still early, and only a few curious patrons straggled through to the back. I had no trouble deflecting them back the way they had come.

"'When the danger had passed, Potter Harry gave me no trouble about the fifteen hundred. He escorted me through a hidden hallway to his office and thanked me for the help, paying me in cash. He also handed me a Cuban cigar out of a small humidor that sat upon a writing desk—occupying one corner of the surprisingly plain office.

"'I shall let your waitress know that your drinks are on us tonight,' he said, wearing a magnanimous smile. 'And here, Raven might appreciate this. Put it on.' He opened a desk drawer and withdrew a small sample vial of cologne, setting it on the desk before me.

fi                          fi                          fi

"By the time I found Raven sitting in a booth to the side of the main club area, the place was bustling with people. As I spotted her and crossed to where she sat, the professor Gwen James was being introduced by one of her colleagues and taking the stage. I paused as she stepped under the lights and began her talk in warm tones: "Good evening. My name is Gwen James. Before I get started, I would like to recognize…" She was stunning. She looked like Jessica Biel playing a young Gloria Steinem, which turned me on in ways I can hardly express. She wore a dark skirt suit that was tailored to accent her athletic curves. She wore a pair of rimless, rectangular, designer glasses, and it was

172

immediately clear why she decided to forego contacts—no one, male or female, would have been able to take that face seriously without them. The glasses allowed her to portray an image that was both sexy and intellectual at the same time. This was a modern feminist reveling in her sexuality.

"I hurried over to Raven, hoping she hadn't seen the open awe with which I had been looking at Ms. James. As I passed the main bar, I saw that one of the three very busy bartenders was that jackass Green. He glanced up and met my eyes in recognition, but immediately looked back down to his work. I tried to dismiss him from my mind. I reached Raven's booth, a semi-circle around a small table, to find her with company. Brandi was there making herself small, in the middle between Raven and a gentleman I'd never met. I suppose Raven pointed me out, because he jumped out of his seat and pumped my hand.

"'Name's Darryl Goodluck, call me Darryl,' he said, smiling.

"'Eben,' I replied.

"'Well, let's sit down,' he said, gesturing.

"I had been hallucinating at a low level since the incident with vampiric Raven in my Honda, but I'd been able to keep it down to a bearable annoyance. For some reason, though, Goodluck threw my mind into complete disarray. All I could do was take my place on the red plastic seat next to Raven and try to get a grip on myself. Goodluck was sitting across from me, but I couldn't look at him directly. Every few seconds or so, his image would flicker in my head. What I could see was bizarre and frightening—he was taking on aspects of horror icons. The hand gripping his drink became Freddy Kreuger's glove of blades, his face the hockey mask of Jason Vorhees, then Gary Oldman as Dracula, Michael Myers, Frankenstein, Voldemort; villains of every stripe. Flick, flick, flick. I kept my focus on Professor James while Goodluck spoke to Raven in hushed tones. When his image finally settled down, I thought it had gotten stuck on *Interview with a Vampire* because Goodluck's face bore an uncanny resemblance to that of Tom Cruise, only Goodluck was taller in stature and rougher of features. He was fifty, give or take a year, and had dark, salt-and-pepper hair. A full head of it; long and pulled back in a ponytail that snaked down his back. His eyes were a very dark blue. He possessed charisma and gravitas in spades, radiating control.

"I immediately disliked him.

"In fact, I think some part of me hated him. Maybe his resemblance to Tom Cruise made me think of Scientology, which reminded me of my experience with the Narc-anon folks with their assists and orgs. Their closed societies and prejudicial behavior. Their silly Galactic Overlord. Maybe it was the way he looked at Raven, and knowing that they'd had a relationship that teed me off. Whatever it was, I tried to swallow it and plastered on a smile.

"Raven seemed happy.

"'Darryl says he knows where my guitar is,' she said, looking at him with hope in her eyes. I looked to Goodluck for confirmation, and he was nodding.

"'I know who has it, and I know how to get it back.' He said. He spoke with a slight twang—a city boy transplanted from the country as a child.

"'Well, let's go get it. Tonight, after the show.' Goodluck was shaking his head.

"'It's not that simple.' He used overemphasized body language in a way that was peculiar to the folk of east Texas and Arkansas. He raised a brow and leaned forward.

"'What do you mean?' I asked.

"'The folks who have it left town. I don't know where they are right this moment, but I do know where they'll be this weekend. And I imagine they'll have the guitar with 'em.' He said guitar with the accent on the first syllable.

"He glanced over his shoulder dramatically, and then withdrew from a pocket a tightly folded piece of colorful, heavy grade paper. He unfolded it, and out from the folds fell a Susan B. Anthony dollar. He proceeded to deftly play the coin along his knuckles like a sleight-of-hand artist. For some reason, this made me hate him even more.

"'And where is that?' I asked. Goodluck may have detected my sentiment, because he looked up at me sharply upon my words. He smoothed the paper on the table and turned it my direction. It was an advertisement for an extreme sports competition. There was a picture of a skater grinding his board on the lip of a half pipe.

"'This is one of them extreme sports events. It's bein' held in Page, Arizona, which is a tourist town up there on the Utah border, not too far from the Grand Canyon. Coupla' the competitors skateboarders—were here the week of yall's—incident. There was an exhibition in Fair Park. Long story short, a crackhead bum named Parker broke into your car and wound up selling the guitar in question to these skaters for a hunnerd dollar bill.'

"'Shit, the Grand Canyon? That's nuts!' I said.

"'Well,' Goodluck grinned with what almost could be called a leer, 'no more nuts'n anything else in this world, I don't guess.'

"I looked at Raven. 'So, what's the plan?'

"Raven parted her lips to answer, but Goodluck jumped in:

"'I'll need ta fly up there tomorrow or Sundee and start gettin' ready for 'em. They should arrive by Thursdee.' He paused for a moment and glanced at Raven, pretending to be unsure of himself.

"'Thing is,' he continued, 'I can't do this thing alone. Too many bases to cover. I need a partner.'

"'I'll go,' Raven chimed in. Goodluck smiled, showing all of his teeth, and a hot feeling flushed through me.

"'No,' I said, as politely as possible. 'You stay here and take care of things. I'll go to Page with Darryl and *we will bring your guitar back.*'

"Goodluck kept smiling and playing his coin over his knuckles, going back and forth between hands.

"'That okay with you?' I asked him.

"'Sure, sure! Long as you can keep a cool head. Hell, you might even learn somethin'!' he said laughing and half-choking on his cocktail.

"One of Potter's employees came and fetched Raven and Brandi so they could get ready for their performance. As Professor Gwen James—being gawked at by every hetero male in the room, including Goodluck and myself—wrapped up her presentation, he and I spoke briefly about whether to leave Saturday or Sunday. The decision was Sunday and I gave him enough cash to purchase the airline tickets. During the intermission we both ordered fresh drinks, and sat without speaking further. I unfocused my eyes and allowed low-grade hallucinations to dance in my peripheral vision, waiting for Raven to take the stage.

22.

"**W**ho can say why some singers become stars with their songs on the lips of millions, while others of equal talent play for a few hundred dollars and free beer in dark, out of the way dives? Argue the merits and demerits of the free market system (the term is a complicated oxymoron) all you wish—one of its chief problems is that it treats artwork the same as it treats any other product. Without music, our world would be a dark and mean place. I think collectively, we benefit from it more than can possibly be measured. Yet we allow corporate behemoths to subtly manipulate the tastes of the masses, not for the enrichment of their minds, nor for their enlightenment, nor indeed for any reason aside from figuring out how to more efficiently separate the folk from their dollars.

"'The way it is' is the mantra, ubiquitous amongst the artists who find themselves in the predicament of catering to the system or not being allowed to do what they love. They have a strong urge to bring some beauty into the world, or some powerful instructive message. Too often though, once their work has been run through the pipes of a corrupted medium, and the artist herself has been banged out of shape in order to suit the vision of some profit machine. She finds that she has become the very thing she had intended to balance. Musicians should get better and more creative as they age, but our system turns them into burnt parrots of their youth after a decade or less of stardom. They offer us medicine for our suffering, and for payment we force feed them a double dose of our sickness.

"A spotlight faded up and revealed Raven sitting on a stool before a microphone. She looked otherworldly, elfin almost, and vulnerable. The crowd watching hushed. She strummed her first chord after looking out and simply saying, 'Hey.' To my surprise, the song she opened with was the one I had teased her about, the haunting and beautiful 'Going Nowhere' by the suicidal Elliott Smith. He spent his youth in Dallas before moving west with his family as a teenager. Dallas may well be his Hell, because I see his ghost here and there, wandering on the streets and looking out through disaffected faces in trashed-out cars and dirty city buses. As Raven deftly moved into the bridge, another spotlight displayed Brandi sitting and playing panpipes in accompaniment. The beautiful tones and perfect melodies of the guitar, pipes, and vocals danced with each other in my mind, and I became entranced. I wasn't alone. The faces I could see in the darkness were as lost as I was in the depths of Raven's bittersweet passion:

> "'The clock moved a quarter of a turn,
> The time it took her cigarette to burn.'"

Eben raised himself up a little, straightening his back, closed his eyes and sang the verse in a quiet, but warm voice. There were tears in his eyes as he stopped and stared, first at his hands, then at the concrete that formed the base of my bunk, upon which I still sat, then up at me and into my eyes. I could feel his thoughts pouring into my skull with the eye contact. Snatches of music and noise snocked into my aural perceptions like static electricity.

"I need another cup," he said, standing to stretch. He took his cup and left my cell. I took the opportunity to use the restroom and make myself another cup as well. Eben returned a few minutes later with his own steaming mug and a fresh bag of oatmeal cookies, offering me a handful. I thanked him, and we sat for a few moments. The only sounds were the crunch of cookies and the slurp of hot coffee. Before long he began again with his tale, his tones heavy and reflective:

"I'm not sure that I ever fell in love with Raven, but my feelings for her certainly changed that night. If anything, oddly enough, it seemed to me that *Raven* the idea in my head became more distant and unattainable, which made me want her all the more.

"I was at least half drunk by the time the wet t-shirt contest ended, and I don't remember much beyond somehow getting Raven to my house and making love to her in a frenzy. I was trying with every twice-intoxicated cell in my body to bridge the ever-widening divide. I was desperate for a connection. I see so easily now what I was blind to at the time."

Eben paused again and looked at me with a conspiratorial gleam in his eyes.

"I found a copy of *Tuesdays With Morrie* in my cell when I moved in. It was in the corner by the shitter. Had to tear off the pissy cover. You ever read it?" he asked me.

"No," I replied after clearing my throat, "heard of it. Some kind of feel-good Oprah deal—wasn't there a movie or something?"

"I don't know," he said. "Probably. I was bored a couple of days ago and read the first half. It's about this old sociology professor who knows he's about to die of uh…cancer, I think. Well, I guess it's really about the guy who wrote the book, Mitch Albom. He's some kind of sports writer. I didn't think I'd ever heard of him (later I realized I had), but that doesn't mean shit. Morrie is the old guy, and he was Mitch's undergrad professor in the late seventies. I guess the guy dies in the mid-nineties sometime. Morrie is some kind of quirky eternal optimist, and he ends up on Nightline with Ted Koppel talking about how he's dying, and how he wants to teach the world something with his death. Mitch, who hadn't been in touch with his old prof since college days, sees the interview and flies out to see the old geezer on his deathbed. A few weeks later, Mitch's newspaper union goes on strike. Now he's out of a job, so he flies back out to see Morrie again.

"This was on a Tuesday, so Mitch starts visiting Morrie every subsequent Tuesday, and *voila*—a bestseller is born. The idea is that Mitch had lost himself somewhere between his heady college days and Morrie's death days. He tried being a piano player in New York City for a while, but that wasn't happening (when I read that, I realized I *had* heard of him. He played keyboard for a while in Stephen King's band of writers the *Rock Bottom Remainders*. I read about them after Albom's feel-good books started selling millions, but Stephen King had described him as '*columnist* Mitch Albom,' a subtle slight that I'm sure Mitch took quite personal indeed, unless I am very much mistaken). So he went back to school and wound up being a big-time sports journalist. He goes out of his way in the book to make the impression that he was some sort of lost soul, trapped by his career. How, through the hustle and bustle of going to sports events, writing about them, interviewing egotistical athletes, and appearing on TV and radio to offer his opinions about some damn sports (for a shitload of money), he had lost sight of the important things in life. And now his dying old teacher, who seems like he was a pretty good guy, was going to remind him and give him life lessons from his deathbed.

"By the second Tuesday, Mitch brings in a tape recorder and tells Morrie he wants to have his voice after he is gone. Can you believe that? I don't know if that's really how it went down, but I'm sure Morrie knew the deal from Jump Street. Mitch was flying seven hundred miles one way to spend time with his dear old prof, whom he hadn't seen, or even called for Christ sake, *at all* for the fifteen years since he'd left school. I'm reading it going, *are you fucking kidding me?* At one point he actually says, 'Morrie was not in the self-help business,' referring to the self-help books flooding the bookshelves at the time, and the absurd number of self-help groups popping up under every loose stone. Yeah, no shit Mitch. The guy has less than six months to live and can't even wipe his own ass. But what about you, huh

180

Mitch? Mitchy, Mitchy, Mitchy. What business are *you* in? You out to save all those workaholics lost and suffering souls, is that it? My hero.

"Admit it, bud. The book was half-written in your head before you ever plunked that tape recorder down in front of the old man. Hell, I'm sure you had your pitch down pat an hour after you saw your old prof on Nightline. I'm guessing the ink was still wet on your book deal while Morrie was breathing his last. It's not the money that makes me taste piss in my mouth — it's the hypocrisy. He went on and on about how screwed up and shallow our culture is. Talked about tabloid news, Princess Di, JFK Jr., O.J. Simpson, and blah, blah, blah. It made me want to puke. This sports writer turns a dying old man into an athlete sliding headfirst onto the point of the reaper's scythe!"

Eben stood and started pacing the three steps that were available to him each way in my cell. He was truly angry, and I was amused. After a time of this, he stopped and said, "Mitch Albom wouldn't know a real problem if it raped him and left him for dead in a lowly shack. Shhuh."

Before I continue, I'd like to reemphasize Eben's angry critique of Mitch Albom's little tome about how Morrie lived and died. The vehemence of his vitriol struck me. As an old man looking back I've found that, as a general rule, when a man gets that perturbed and angry over something he sees in another — in this case, Albom's hypocrisy it's because he shares this very trait, and the anger is really (as it almost always is) a defense mechanism. I knew at that moment that to call Eben Thomas a hypocrite would be tantamount to an open declaration of war — despite the fact that in some ways he is a hypocrite, or, at the least, believes himself to be one.

Eben paced some more, and I let him cool down. He was unstable. I could see that clearly. He was full of angst, resentment, disgust and — something else. Something traumatic. The potency of his emotions held me fast. It came across in waves of red and amber *creamy heat* that flowed from his forehead and chest. I couldn't have possibly uttered a word at that moment. I was entranced by something far deeper than words. I would have waited quiet hours for him to continue his story. Only a few minutes passed, though, before he came back to himself and settled to the floor and his coffee. He took a deep breath and spoke on the exhale:

## 23

Eben sat back down and began speaking, but stopped after two words. He was more deeply disturbed than I had thought. I held up my old brown hand.

"Why don't we take a break? Neither of us are going anywhere anytime soon, I don't think."

Eben looked at me with eyes that were almost feral in their intensity. When he looked away, they didn't lose any of their wildness, but the focus shifted inward. He looked as though he were trying to square some irrational truth.

"Okay," he said. He arose again from his seat on the concrete floor and gathered his coffee implements, "Tomorrow morning."

I nodded my head and waved him off. He opened and shut my cell door as quietly as he could manage. I rummaged in my property bag and came out with an orange I had saved from breakfast a few days before, and a book I had found that I hadn't read in decades.

I peeled the orange and carefully laid the pieces out on a piece of paper on my steel desk. I looked at the cover of the book. It was *The Two Towers*, part of J.R.R. Tolkien's *The Lord of the Rings* trilogy. Before I started reading, I thought about how strange it was that I had stumbled upon the second book here in jail. It was strange because it just so happened that the second installment of Peter Jackson's motion picture depiction of the series was the only one of the three that I had seen. I was bored several years ago and walked into a movie theater, the dollar movies I believe, up in Garland. I picked *The Two Towers* by default. It was the only decent-looking movie playing within the hour. I had read the books sometime in the eighties, and I struggled to remember the storyline as I watched.

None of that mattered very much, odd as it was, as I opened the book and began to read. I was hoping for a diversion, both from Eben's story, which had me completely in its grip, and the monotony of the cell. I read, turned pages, ate when they brought a meal, and eventually fell asleep with the book open on my bare chest.

## 24.

I wasn't out of the woods yet. My half-delirious memories and visions of Eli had gotten me through the worst of the pain. But, my healing in that dark hole, located Devil-knows-where in the byzantine maze that is the Dallas County Jail, took weeks, months—I don't know. I had only a very weak grasp on my sense of the passage of time. The old man, whose name I never learned, unceasingly brought my food and water, occasionally another syrette of morphine (though that was rare), or a few Tylenol 3s, or just regular Tylenol. Every bit of it was like manna from heaven. I'd croak out a thank you every time he'd come. I'd make sure and conserve enough energy to at least offer meager thanks for his kindnesses. His day off was Sunday, and his replacements would just shove the food through the bean chute, not caring whether it spilled out onto the floor. The old man always returned, though. He was there the entire time. I wonder, looking back, why the old man was doing so much time in county. I never asked him that either. Could have been anything. He could have been a mass murderer for all I knew, or on some maxed-out misdemeanor sentence. I don't know.

I was in such a broken mental state that, if I'd been weaker or older, I'm sure I would have kicked the bucket there in that miserable dark. Dead Ezekiel. I had no fight in my will, but my body disagreed with the sentiments of my mind—that it was perhaps time to die. Eli's face and words circled throughout my head amongst other disparate fragments of sense and perception. Memories. Dreams. Some days, hours, moments, were good, and I felt optimism through the pain. Other days, minutes, lifetimes, were horrifying. I wanted to die. I would weep quietly, listening to the other inmates in their successive holes yell and scream at each other, or scream and kick at the walls and doors. Three or four of them had a chess tournament going, each of them with a rigged up chess set in their cells. They would call out their moves at all hours of the day or night, sometimes getting in vituperative arguments over the rules or the placement of the pieces.

I never spoke to the others. Never uttered a single word to them, though there were times when we would repeat our ghastly communal screams and laughter. At some point, the others got word of what I had done to the Mexican kid. They yelled questions out to me but I never answered. I heard things like "I'm go' whoop you like ol' boy dahn thah whooped that other spic you ol' Mexican-talkin' bitch!"

I heard the story told several times, though some of the stories were out of dreams, I think. I heard that the kid was dead. Or no, that he didn't have a scratch on him, that he had almost killed *me*. Or that his face was permanently scarred—*I believed that*. One guy even said that they had had to amputate one of the kid's arms. The more I think about it, the surer I am that much of what I heard was a dream. It was more than a dream, even. It was the *cream* taking hold of me, just as it had been doing with my visions of Eli.

A man with a low and gravelly voice that seemed to carry through the concrete told the amputation story. All else was quiet while he recounted his version of events, and I mustered my will to focus on what he was saying. His words were nonsensical—most of them anyway—and he digressed in the middle of my attack on the kid to an experience he had on an Amtrak train in Northern Florida. The train, so he said, derailed, crashed and killed everyone aboard aside from himself (he got out with a broken "thalax" he said. I still don't believe there is such a body part) and an eight-year-old boy (who had only a "small cut upon the buttocks" were his words). The boy took the man behind the voice by the hand and led him to a suitcase that contained thirty thousand, one-dollar bills. It had apparently belonged to his now-dead parents. He wound back around to my story, and said that after beating the Mexican kid "up and down death's sidewalk," I started *chewing* on the kid's forearm, biting chunks of flesh out of it, swallowing them, and *slurping at the blood*. The gravelly voice got lower and lower as it depicted this gruesome event until it seemed as though it must have reached an inaudible register. Such was the sound of the voice that by the time he finished the telling, I would have sworn that he was there in my cell with me. I remember searching the darkness with my eyes—nothing. No one. I imagined glimpses of a demoniac face, but it was fancy. It surely was.

That set of feelings and thoughts tells me that it was *the cream* at work. The biting of the flesh is also an indicator, as it foreshadows the subsequent dream.

It was that same day, or perhaps night—I couldn't tell for certain, that a high fever stole over my wracked body. It was sudden and harsh in the way it hit me, like a physical blow. It didn't surprise me—just another misery stacked upon the heap of miseries that my existence had become. I shivered. My mouth and chin shook. I curled up in a ball on my thin mat on the floor, clasping my filthy sheet to me and sensing that my thoughts were breaking up into delirium.

At length, whatever was going on in my mind coalesced into something resembling consciousness again. It was 'round about this time that the idea occurred to me that I had indeed died, and now I was in hell. A scream of denial burst forth from my chest as I contemplated the possibility that my soul had been

187

found guilty, and that I now tasted the beginnings of an existence of eternal torment. Throughout my life, I disbelieved the idea of hell. Why would a supreme being create the beautiful souls of men, and then condemn the vast majority of his precious creations to a never-ending existence of pain, humiliation, and degradation? Or even to the dark absence of love and goodness, as some philosophers have deemed damnation? After those desperate moments in that accursed hole, my faith changed in character. In a world where such suffering as I had undergone in my mind exists, there is undoubtedly room for the cruel reality of eternal torment. I have no convictions about this—only experience. And in my long years I have found that experience more often serves to deconstruct those things we say we "know" than affirm them. Such is the mystery of our bizarre world, or mine anyway. The wisest of old heads, if they lay upon their death pillows with any clarity, will admit profound and complete ignorance should they choose honesty over compassion.

I wasn't in hell. At least, I don't believe I was. If I was, then I still am and the Great Committee of Torment is having a delicious time meting out my punishment—setting me up for more and more elaborate falls as eternity carries onward. I don't believe this to be the case, despite the fact that me existing in hell is just as plausible an explanation for all of this than any other I could argue. In any event, I wasn't in the type of horrifying hell that I had desperately imagined myself. But, it was during the course of my fever that I had the dream or vision, bursting with *cream*, of the memory of an event that I seldom visit in my head. A memory that I have never spoken of to anybody, including my uncles—three of whom shared the experience.

## 25.

I wasn't one hundred percent sure that I would write this event here, seen through a series of dark glasses, until now—though it had clouded my mind while I wrote the story of my dreams of Eli. Eben has taken his price from me. There is no doubt about it now, and there is also no doubt that there is more to come with Eben. It may well be that I have taken my price from him as well. That price is this story—his, and mine. My story of *he cream* would be incomplete were it lacking the events that occurred in the woods south of Mt. Pleasant, Texas. I experienced them as a vision in a delirious fever dream, lying in that dark cell. That place is now a blackened tumor in my brain, spreading deceit and madness along every pathway it encounters.

As I said, my thoughts had fragmented and then reformed as fear, mental fear, as it were: paranoia. From there, I came to a place of surreal clarity. This is why I say it was a vision *or* a dream—I can't for sure say which—on account of me unable to tell whether I was conscious or not.

As I lay there, it had only been a matter of months since this nightmare had occurred in reality. I was trying to block what I had seen and heard (and smelled—that was the worst, I think) from my mind, to shove it deep into my unconscious troves. The sense of clarity that came over me was a removal, or breach, of those blocks and defenses. I am sure of that, and the memory rushed through my mind like a noxious, inexorable river:

It was five or six months prior to the incident with Darryl and Lexi that had landed me in jail, and in Mexican-maiming rage. I was alone in my room at the Tampico, lying in bed, dreaming. The dual dream resonated. The dream of a dream was a wakefulness. The phone rang and awoke me.

"Yeah?" I said into the receiver.

"Get ready," it was Big Dog, my terse uncle. "We coming to pick you up, we got work."

"A'ight," I rejoined.

My uncles were my business partners. They supplied nearly all of the drugs I sold, and they had their hands in all sorts of moneymaking enterprises. All but one or two of which were criminal: dog—and cock—fighting, moonshine and bootlegging, fencing stolen property. Whatever, really. Slim even had a girl running four "candy houses" in the projects and other run-down apartment buildings. She sold stolen candy, sodas, and other knick-knacks—school supplies, shit like that—to neighborhood kids. A regular ghetto Robin Hood. The money was flowing, and my uncles felt like they were in high-cotton, gangster heaven. This was before gangsta' rap turned every halfway-smart, inner-city, black kid into a wannabe. The mid to late eighties was their hey-day, and they were throwing their weight around in West Dallas, South Dallas, and Oak Cliff. I stayed out of most of their business, but it was expected that if they needed me I'd be available to them. No-questions-asked-period.

I shook the sleep off and washed my face. I dressed, loaded my pistol, put it in my waistband and waited. Before long, I heard the honk of a horn outside. I turned off the squawk box and hit the door.

I got into the back seat of a car I'd never seen before: a mid-seventies model Lincoln, long and wide. It was a real land barge designed, built and sold in the years just prior to OPEC's fuel shenanigans that tripled gas prices and gave birth to the term "gas guzzler." It was no surprise that they would be in a strange car. My uncles were always buying and selling cars. Larry had a dealer's license and they went to the auction almost every week.

Three of my uncles were in the car. James, the undisputed Alpha of the family, was in the back seat with me. In the past few years, everybody had taken to calling James "Big Dog," which was as apt an appellation as I have ever come across. He was a huge man, six-feet five and over three hundred pounds. He was fat, no question about that, but he carried it stolidly. He always had the look on his face of being in control, and this day was no exception. He said nothing as I climbed into the back seat next to him. Larry, almost as big a man as Big Dog, was driving, and Joseph, whom they called Slim because he was the only one of my five living uncles who wasn't overweight, was in the front passenger seat.

If Big Dog was quiet and kept his own counsel, Slim was the very opposite. He was the quintessential, fly, black man of the seventies, though now he'd taken on the hip-hop flair of the eighties. Slim was one of those rare and annoying people who always seem to be talking. It was almost as if his greatest fear was the vacuum in his mind that would occur if he stopped the chatter. I detested Slim, and the feeling was mutual. Out of all my uncles he picked on me most during my youth, and I had never forgiven him. Still haven't. I got drunk one night—shit, years ago—maybe a few months after he died, and pissed on his grave. Every time he was around at Big Mommas he was all over me for reading books and learning how to speak well. "Actin' white," he called it. Like getting an education was a betrayal of my race. I hated that attitude then, and I still hate it. That was what he did to me in the open. The reason I pissed on his grave was what he had done in private, back in my room. That's one part of my life I'm not going into, and it only happened twice. I don't know why I didn't kill him. We never talked about it when I got older, and we both pretended like it never happened. I pretended that he just didn't exist, and he obliged my sentiment. Son-of-a-bitch probably thought I had forgotten. I don't know. I don't care.

"What's up, nephew?" Larry said, looking back. I nodded my head in reply.

It was dark. The night sky was covered in low clouds in all directions, as far as the eye could see in the gloom. In my dreaming and visioning mind the clouds writhed with an unnatural life. They were too low, too close, and moving too fast. I felt as if I couldn't breathe. Larry pulled the Lincoln out onto East Grand Avenue and then onto Interstate 30 going east, out of town.

The radio was on Soul (Sockin') 73, but turned low almost to the point of inaudibility. The dream, *the cream*, distorted the music. Instead of the words of the songs, the singers were chanting in Church Latin, "*abyssus abyssum invocat, abyssus abyssum invocat*," and I could see James Brown dressed in a priestly frock. He was dancing wildly, sweating, making the sign of the cross with the movements of his feet like he was dancing in salt. All of this in quietness, though. All of this in the utmost of quietness, so that the true memory played out on its course.

I said nothing. I was the low man on the totem pole, and it was not my place to speak. Big Dog would let me know what I needed to know when the time came. We passed through Mesquite, home of the rodeo, and then into Rockwall, where there are three sections of wall that, if manmade, are the oldest known structures made by man in the world. Then finally we travelled onto the long bridge that crosses over Lake Ray Hubbard. I lost myself looking into the black water out the window when—

"Shit!" I said, startled. Something had bumped my back *hard* through the cushion of the back seat. I rose up and looked behind me as if I expected to see something. Big Dog's face went hard as he looked around outside the Lincoln.

"Pull over," he said.

"Here?" asked Larry.

"Naw, back in Mesquite, fool. What you thank?"

Larry slowed the huge car and pulled it onto the shoulder. Again, the seat jumped with a blow from the other side of it. I had by this time realized that there was a person in the trunk. Big Dog took a tire iron that had been laying at his feet into his monstrous hands and exited the vehicle.

"Pop it when I'm back there," Big Dog said to Larry, who nodded solemnly. I didn't follow directly with my eyes, but I watched in peripheral as my uncle reached the his goal.

"A'ight!" he yelled.

The trunk lock made a *pop* and Big Dog raised the crowbar above his head. I looked through the back windshield, under the raised trunk lid, but I couldn't see the person. Big Dog made a *grunt* as he came down with his weapon without even a second's pause. I winced as the steel on flesh made a *thump* and the car jumped a little on its suspension with the man's movements. The man was tied up and gagged of course, my uncles were not amateurs. The back seat bumped again as he kicked it. Big Dog reached his left hand into the trunk to hold the man steady, and *thump*—he came down with the crowbar again. This time, the car jumped once before all went quiet and still.

"Goddam," said Slim. "*Goddam.*"

Big Dog remained back there for fifteen seconds, or so, with his hands in the trunk. He then shut it and made his way back to the seat next to me. His breathing was heavy.

"Let's go," he barked. Larry pulled the Lincoln, still running, back onto the highway. "You know what them white folk'll do to us, they get us pulled over out here."

My heart was pounding. The dream/vision made the blur of the outside look a vast wasteland. The night's shadows and the dark clouds threw everything I could see into stark relief against the bright objects that came like slow strobe-flashes into the path of our headlights. We passed over Lake Ray Hubbard, and into east Texas proper—a.k.a. *Bumpkinsville*. My uncle was right: black folks, especially black men from the city, were not welcome out here. Not welcome, and certainly not after sundown. As a boy growing up around older black friends and neighbors, I heard all about "Sundown Towns," where signs openly said: *"Do not let the sun go down on you."* "You" meaning blacks. In ninety-five percent of the white minds in a racist-ass town like that, including the police, the word would be "nigger," of course. My uncle's decision to bring us out here shocked me. I knew he wasn't stupid, so there had to be a good reason. The question must have been written all over my face because Big Dog spoke:

"It's A.J.," he said. I was flabbergasted.

"The Jamaican?"

Big Dog nodded. I could barely think. The Jamaicans had been bringing massive amounts of cocaine into South Dallas over the past couple of years. They were selling most of it in the new, smokable formulation of crack. This was smack in the middle of the infamous "crack epidemic." Everybody in the hood seemed to be smoking it, and whoever had it was getting paid big time. In Dallas, as in several cities at the time, the Jamaicans were the ones who had it..

One thing about those dreadlock-sporting fools was that they stuck together, and they already garnered a reputation as being cruel, violent killers who used automatic weapons, and couldn't be trusted. We did business with them, but we hated them. I say "we," just lumping myself with my uncles. I personally didn't deal with them much. I rarely sold crack, and never smoked it. I sensed early on that the drug was going to be a big problem. None of us dreamed of how big it would eventually become—ravaging entire neighborhoods, giving police and politicians the perfect excuse to lock up two generations of black men. I knew even then that it was the kind of trouble I didn't want.

"What the fuck?" I said.

"A.J. and his bitch-ass boys hit one of our powder houses, over offa Ann, night befo' last. They shot L.T. Killt 'im."

"Damn."

"Naw. Just so happened, we had two keys chillin' at that house. They was only there for a coupla' hours and was about ta be moved. Well, I guess L.T. tol' 'em where it was at, an' they got it."

I sat in silence, waiting for him to continue. Big Dog always took pauses when speaking at length, sometimes for a minute or more at a time.

"L.T. was smokin' crack, anyway. He didn't know we knew. It's partially my fault fah not pullin' his ass."

He paused again, rubbing the back of his neck, as he often would during these pauses. Slim turned his head and looked as though he would chime in, but a look from Big Dog stayed his tongue.

"They may've gotten away with this shit, but they didn't know– we had jus' put in a video security system at that house. They was cameras on the doors and in the livin' room. We put 'em in so's the workers could destroy the dope in a bucket of acid in the floor of the back closet if the cops hit. We wasn't too worried 'bout...anyway, these muthafuckin' Jamaicans..."

"Shit," said Slim, shaking his head. Big Dog paused again, his eye on his smaller brother.

"They never did see the cameras. They was wearin' masks, but A.J.'s big, ugly ass dreadlocks gave him away. We fount his ass this afternoon. He wouldn't tell us where the shit was at, so we started cuttin' on him. He started talkin' then. Larry gave him some o' that truth serum shit, too, but that was a big ass mess. He finally tol' us it was out here in mothafuckin' East Texas. They got some kinda spot out here in tha damn sticks.

"Truth serum?" I asked. "That shit real?"

"Aw, hell yeah. It ain't nuttin' but some strong ass barbs. Sodium Pentothal. It was bullshit, though. He was blubberin' nonsense half the time. Pissed on hisself. Info we're goin' on is from when we was cuttin'. We used the drugs to confirm what he was sayin'. I guess it was good enough fah that." Pause.

"He knows he gon' die if he don' come up wi' the shit. Shit..." He trailed off. A hard look remained on his face.

195

I sat back in my seat, contemplating what I had just heard. My dream world expanded and contracted with the drama of it, like a lung breathing in and out, in and out. Darkness took my vision down to a tiny point of light, and then the light expanded out into the shadows flashing by at seventy miles per hour. I steeled my resolve. It took only a few minutes of quiet thought to grasp the reality of my situation. No matter how this played out, I was about to be party to a murder. They weren't going to make me pull the trigger, but there was no question as to whether our Jamaican friend would be surviving his predicament. None at all. My uncle was right, though. Even if A.J. was smart enough to realize that we were going to kill him, he would still cling to any hope that was offered him. A false chance was better than no chance, as illogical as that sounds. The coke probably was out here in the woods of east B.F.E., as A.J. had given.

## 26

*These men lie in wait for their own blood; they ambush
only themselves!*

—*Proverbs 1*

Time was suspended in the dream/vision. My memory told me
that we rode on in quietness. The radio fuzzing into pink and
brown noise that played accompaniment to Ray Charles, Nat
King Cole and Billie Holiday—my dream gave me long
stretches of ghost noise.

The next event came on, in my vision, in stages: as if the
pressure and stress of it sent waves into its past, echoes of great
shock overlapped the tranquility and were gone. Overlapped,
then gone. The shock grew stronger with each wave, the
quietness weaker. Pop-Pop-POP-*pop*-Pop- POP-*pop*-Pop-POP!

A gunshot went off in the cab of the Lincoln! We were
going over sixty miles per hour along an empty stretch of
Interstate Thirty—seventy or eighty miles east of Dallas. Hell
exploded all at once, as no one knew what had happened. Larry
lost control of the Lincoln, and we tumbled into a field of grass

that ran along the highway. We spun around in circles. Everyone in the car was yelling, and after ten heart-rending seconds, Larry was somehow able to regain control, slamming on the brakes. We came to rest in the field, between two trees. We had missed them both by a matter of inches.

As soon as, if not a bit before, the land barge came to a complete stop, all four of us running on instinct and adrenaline, jumped out of our respective doors and drew our pistols.

"The fuck was that?!" yelled Slim. "Goddam, what the fuck?"

We just stood there breathing hard, looking at each other. Checking ourselves.

"Anybody shot?" Big Dog asked the group. "Somebody's gun go off?"

"Nope."

"Naw."

I shook my head. I thought back to the event. What had I seen? I was in a sort of a trance—a reverie—when all of a sudden…

"It came from the trunk," I said. I had remembered a white flash of some sort of fabric or plastic going by, between Big Dog and me. I said so to my uncles. Big Dog hadn't seen it, but it was really the only option left on the table. How does it go? "…Whatever is left, however unlikely…"

"How'd he get a fuckin' gun?" said Slim. "What the hell? *This* muthafuckah's a goddam Houdini. I seen it all nah. What the hell we go' do? I got—"

A car passed on the highway, headlights briefly illuminating the scene.

"Hush, fool. Shit, we gotta get outta here. Fuck it, pop the trunk. He's got ta be still tied up. Got ta be."

There were no subsequent shots. His hands had been tied with rope and tape behind his back. However he had gotten hold of the gun, he would have to be in an awkward position to shoot out when we opened the trunk lid. Big Dog walked quietly over to where Larry stood, leaned close to him, and spoke words I couldn't make out. The blood was rushing through my system, roaring in my ears. My heart was struggling to calm down. Big Dog gesticulated at Slim and me to move back. We did so, shuffling backwards still holding our pistols. Big Dog crept up to the passenger side of the trunk, behind the wheel well, and crouched down. Larry stepped over to the open driver door. He reached in, slow and steady. First, he quietly pushed in the knob on the dash that killed the headlights. All went dark. The only light that remained was that of the dome in the cab, and a dim ambience that shone from a distant lamppost.

Big Dog help his pistol in his right hand, and had as serious an expression on his face as I have ever seen on a man. It was the expression of a man who was prepared to deal death; one that I have since worn myself, more than once. The trunk *popped* and rose an inch. Big Dog didn't move. Nothing happened. I tried to envision what A.J. was doing in there. Was he even conscious? Were his bonds still in place? Did he still have the gun? Were there any more bullets in it? Questions bounced about in my head as if they were printed on the front pages of newspapers in huge bold letters. Larry went to a knee and pointed his gun at the trunk.

Ten seconds passed. Fifteen. Thirty. The dream/vision made all of the objects I could see look surreal. The shadows were cast at conflicting angles. The chirp of cricket bows and the rasp of cicadas harmonized with the faint sound of the radio. I struggled to keep a grasp on the timeline. The Jamaican's face began popping into my consciousness. I could see his blood, fat drops of it, on the browned leaves and sticks that covered the floor of the woods. A campfire crackled. More echoes of the future. A.J.'s Jamaican voice, the violence and fear in it was dissonant with the peace and confidence in Eli's Jamaican voice. Eli's face replaced that of A.J. "*Fallacy,*" he groaned, blood dripping from the corner of his mouth. "*Understanding fallacy is understanding yourself.*"

A minute passed, and the tension grew with every heartbeat. *What was Big Dog's plan?* I didn't know. I imagined A.J. bursting from the trunk. In my mind's eye he jumped up, pistol trained on me. I couldn't lift my gun. It was so heavy. I couldn't move! Another long minute passed, and a crackly song ended.

Without warning, the trunk slammed open, and A.J.s slim, dark form emerged. His hands were free! How had he gotten free? So many questions. The event lasted a mere matter of seconds. In the dark, from a perspective thirty feet away, it was a blur. A.J. raised the gun and turned, but away from where Big Dog crouched. Big Dog lunged and grabbed the much smaller man's arm. *Pop! Pop!* The gun barked, and flashes sent colors into my vision. I could see very little. I heard my uncle's grunt of effort, and then a yell from A.J. The gun reported once more, and then I could see Big Dog pull A.J. out of the trunk by his long, greasy hair. He seemed to handle the smaller man as if he were a child. There was a swift movement, and then the unmistakable sound of A.J.'s soft head being slammed into the hard metal of the Lincoln's body. A.J. went to the ground in a limp heap.

"A'ight," said Big Dog. We all approached the scene. "Put him in the back seat, in the middle. Let's go!"

Larry and I did as we were bid. A.J., a bag of bones, was between Big Dog and me. We were back on the Interstate less than two minutes later, all four of us breathing hard. At least one of my uncle's breaths stank like a dead rat's butthole, and A.J. smelled as though he had both pissed and shit himself, as well as not having showered for at least a week. I rolled the window down for some clean, cool night air. Slim handed back two fat rolls of tape. I held a gun on our comatose prisoner while my uncle re-bound and gagged his stinking ass.

A.J. was concussed. He was bleeding from the ears. I knew there was a good possibility that he wouldn't wake up again. He was completely unconscious—making no sounds, no moves. I held the gun on him anyway, and with vigilance. I wasn't about to trust my senses when it came to a man who had been able to break similar bonds (I'm sure my uncle's had been meticulous), and come up with a firearm. That fucker Slim was right. This son-of-a-bitch was Houdini MacGyver, P.I. I almost hated to see talent like that wasted. Almost.

Again, *the cream* folded time. I remember a sign for Mt. Pleasant and turning off onto a farm road that wound like an asphalt serpent out into the countryside. It soon became a tiny road that skirted a forest of low trees: cedars, evergreens, here and there. A taller Live Oak rose head and shoulders above the rest, like a serene shepherd tending his flock.

"There's the creek," said Slim. He was consulting a map with directions scrawled in one corner. After the creek, we turned onto a dirt road that led into the woods. The radio had phased into all crackles and noise. Neither of my uncles in the front turned it off—nerves, I guessed. *The cream* was speaking to me. Fear jabbering. The hanging tree limbs were claws grasping at the Lincoln, scraping it with high-pitched *screeks.*

"Kill the lights," said Big Dog.

"Cain't see shit," Larry rejoined.

"Do it and slow the fuck down."

Larry pushed in the knob that turned off the headlights. All went pitch black. He slowed the car to a crawl, and before long our eyes adjusted to the gloom. We could make out the trees and the lighter color of the dirt road. Larry was the only one of us who wore glasses, and he was squinting through them, but seemed to be able to stay on the road. Pre-memories of fire light danced through my head. A.J.'s face snarling, blood. Then Eli's face again, pacific. "Let me tell you about Nietzsche and his super-man, and you tell me if you can find anything wrong about his thinking." Then, it was Nietzsche himself, sitting alone at the campfire. His eyes were gazing far away, rocking back and forth—his mind overcome by desire for a woman he couldn't have.

"E," Big Dog said.

"Yeah."

"C'mon, let's get this fool out."

We had stopped. I could just barely make out the dark shape of an old cabin. It was small—either two small rooms, or one larger one—and seemingly empty. There were no lights. No cars. Our prisoner was still out cold. We carried him to the

201

cabin. Big Dog and I stood over him while Larry and Slim searched the place with flashlights. Their report just confirmed what we could easily see. The cabin was empty aside from two rollaway cots, an empty dresser that was falling apart, and a few canned goods on a rickety shelf. That was in the back room. In the front was an old couch, a table and nothing else other than a framed print of a painting of an orchid. It hung at a strange angle on the wall. The old cabin was dusty, but there were signs that it had recently been occupied. Someone had swept the floor with the broom leaning against the wall. No sign of any cocaine.

"We gotta wake his Jamaican ass up," said Big Dog. He looked around, stepped outside and then came back in.

"Slim, Larry," he said. "There's some wood and a fire pit out there. Lighter fluid, too. Start a fire—not too big, fool. Use four or five pieces of that wood, put some twigs and little shit under it and light that."

They went. Big Dog and I picked A.J. up and carried him out a few minutes later. The campfire of my *creamy* pre-memory had become a reality. It crackled, and the sounds of the woods harmonized: an owl hooted, something rustled nearby, and my inexperienced imagination wondered if some predator was stalking us. I made sure the safety was off on my pistol. I'm a city boy, born and raised. I didn't know anything about cougars and wolves and still don't. I thought there might be bears out there, too. I wasn't sure. The fear babbled on. Time got jumbled. *The cream* was painting strange pictures for me, coalescing in the shadows.

When I looked back down at reality, my uncles had A.J. taped to a chair four or five feet away from the fire. Big Dog had a butcher knife in his hand, and he was holding the tip to the flames.

"E, you watch out and make sure no goddam cougrahs or coyotes run up on our ass. They smell this blood and they may go crazy. And listen for any car engines."

"A'ight."

I held my pistol tight and watched the trees. Wings

flapped, and bushes rustled. The branches took on the look of claws again. *The cream* wound through my head. I fancied I could hear Nietzsche's voice babbling German nonsense to his sister in the cabin. Whatever it was that he said sounded like "sex and suicide, sex and suicide," and maybe that is what he was saying. And then it sounded like his sister replied with, "Shit Freddy, shit..."

"AAARRRGGHH!!"

I turned my head at the yell. Big Dog had taken the red-hot butcher knife to A.J.'s arm. That brought him back to consciousness all right. I caught the scent of cooking flesh. A.J. leaned forward as far as his bonds would allow, and he puked between his legs. Some of the vomit landed in the fire and added to the disgusting smell.

"A'ight, negro. Where the shit at?"

A.J. looked around him. I saw the expression on his face change more than once as he remembered the last several hours of his life. He recognized the cabin and saw where he was. He swayed in his seat. Near the fresh wound on his arm, which was already cauterized, were several slightly older cuts. They had broken open and were running blood down and behind where his hands were tightly bound. Blood stained the front of the man's shirt and jeans as well. It would be easier to single out the parts of his body that weren't somehow injured. One of his eyes was swollen shut, but he finally fixed the other one on Big Dog, standing near enough for whispers still gripping the knife.

"Fuck you," A.J. spat with a glob of blood and saliva into the fire. Big Dog got a gleam in his eyes that I didn't recognize at the time, but that I have seen many times since—the gleam of sadistic pleasure.

Big Dog stepped up to A.J. and cut the Jamaican's shirt open. He then held the knife to the flames again. After a short time, he motioned to Larry who had a gag ready. Larry wrapped tape around A.J.'s biting mouth, and stepped back. I could barely watch what followed, I tried to focus on scanning the trees, but a macabre fascination drew my attention back. Big Dog began slicing the flesh of A.J.'s chest, stomach, and ribs, making deep furrows with the hot metal. Some of the wounds cauterized immediately, others bled profusely. The Jamaican screamed—or tried to—through the tape. He panted and bucked, forcing Larry and Slim to each take a side of him while Big Dog continued his grizzly work. Whatever they had done before could have been nothing compared to this. My uncle was fileting the man. Left untreated, the wounds would be his death from blood loss in a matter of hours. I doubted he would be living anywhere near an hour more, though. I was sweating and breathing hard. A rustle in the woods to my left made me jerk my weapon up. I peered into the gloomy, shifting shadows. Nothing. I looked back. A.J. was nodding his head.

Larry unwrapped the tape.

"Okay, Okay, Okay!" screamed our torture victim. "No more, no more, no more." He was babbling, blood and vomit dibbling from his lips.

"One mo' time, fool, or you die. Where the shit at?"

"Okay. Under da painting of da f-f-flower—der is a loose board on de wall! At de floor, mon! Iss in der, I swear! Ahh!"

Big Dog nodded at Slim, who was already on his way into the cabin. He came back a tense minute or two later, carrying a yellow backpack. He opened the pack in the light of the fire, and drew out a fat lozenge of heavily wrapped plastic.

"That's it," said Slim.

"Where the other one at?" queried Big Dog, looking hard at the dying man. A.J. was crying now, desperate. The pain had made him delirious.

"It's gone, mon. Gonesy. I'm sor-ree. I'm sure most of it is sold by now. Mon, m-m-mon, I'm sor-ree! Please!"

"Put it in the car," said Big Dog. He turned his huge body back to A.J.'s pathetic form.

"You know I'm s'posed to kill you now, right?"

"No! No, mon! C'mon, mon! I tell you where the shit is at, mon! In Dallas, in Dallas, at my cousin house. I swear! I show you!"

"Naw, I don't b'lieve that shit. You was tellin' the truth the first time. I'm surprised we got this much back."

204

"Loo-Look, mon. I go back! I go back to Jamaica. You take me to the airport, you t-t-take me to Miami. I swear I go back! You n-n-never see me again."

"You wanna live?"

My uncle's face was diabolical. I was shivering even though the air was warm and humid. It felt more like Louisiana than Texas. A.J. was weak from blood loss and shock already, I could see it in his face. He was strong, but fading.

"Yes! Yes!" A.J.'s one halfway good eye went huge with hope. His earlier insolence was gone as if it had never been. His only desire was to please my uncle, to convince him to let him live. "Please! I go b-b-back, I swear, mon. Big Dog, I swear!"

"Okay, fool. I'll let you live." Pause. A.J. was *smiling* up at my uncle, of all things. I couldn't believe it. "But you fucked up, man. You got to pay if I'm gon' let you make it."

A.J. looked around, and into the woods, as if he had heard or seen something. He looked back up at Big Dog.

"I got it. I got money! C-c-cash! In Dallas, mon. I pay you!"

"Naw."

Big Dog turned and walked over to the wood pile. Lying next to it was a rusty hand axe. He picked it up and walked back over to A.J.

"Here what you gotta do, A.J. If you wanna live, you got ta eat your finger."

"Wh-What?"

His eye went wide again, this time in fear and misapprehension. I felt my mouth drop open. *What did he say?* My mind went blank. There was another rustle in the woods, this time in a different spot. I raised my weapon—this took my mind off what I had heard, but for only a second or two.

"Gag him and undo his hands."

Larry gagged A.J. and unwrapped the tape on his hands. This took more than a minute. A.J. just sat there in mute shock. I tried to imagine myself in his shoes, and my mind recoiled from the effort.

"You got two choices, A.J. You undahstand? You can either sit there and let me cut your finger offa you, and then you eat it, and maybe you survive all this, or I just kill ya. You wanna live? Some folks would jus' rather die, I undahstand that. Jus' nod ya head if ya wanna live, if you wanna pay my price."

A.J. looked at my uncle in utter disbelief. He even looked over at me, as if I had an answer for him.
"Well?"

Finally, after looking down at the ground and throwing up again, he raised his head, closed his eye, and nodded once, very slowly. His whole body was shaking.

So was mine, though I managed to hide it. Larry looked on stoically, his big hands on A.J.'s shoulders. Slim was smiling, mirroring Big Dog. Big Dog stood a piece of wood up next to A.J. He took the Jamaican's hand and put the middle finger flat on the wood, the rest of the fingers hanging down. A.J. pulled the hand back.

"Ah!" said Big Dog.

Eye still closed, A.J. reluctantly held his hand back out, and Big Dog repeated the process. Satisfied, he reared back with the axe. A.J. continued to shake, his eye squenched shut, blood trickling from his mouth, but he held his finger on the wood. Big Dog came down hard, severing the finger and embedding the axe in the wood. A.J. made another muffled scream and drew both of his hands into his body. He bucked, and Larry had his hands full keeping the Jamaican upright. He finally settled, and Big Dog took up a roll of tape and wrapped the newly crippled hand. He told Larry to remove the gag.

Big Dog gingerly picked up the man's severed digit using thumb and forefinger. The thing was grotesque. I was disgusted and enrapt. The finger jerked in Big Dog's grasp. He dropped it with a curse.

"What the fuck?"

Slim began to laugh. "Goddam, big bro. You scurred of a

lil' finger? Watch out! It might jus' latch on to ya, never let go! Hahaha!"

He picked it up again. This time it didn't move. He showed it to the Jamaican.

"Nah. You wanna live?" He put the thing in A.J.'s shaking hand.

"Eat it. Chew it. Swallah that muthahfuckah!"

A.J. put the finger in his mouth and bit down. I winced. This was the most horrifying thing I had ever seen or imagined. It was a nightmare. I felt as though I was paralyzed. I couldn't move an inch; could barely breath.

"Chew it!" yelled my uncle. Slim laughed again.

I lost it when I heard the crunch of bone. I puked in the other direction from the scene, back towards the car. Again, there was a rustle in the woods, but I saw nothing. I wiped my mouth on my sleeve. That's when I noticed that the fire had died down to mere embers. My uncle continued his torture.

"You best swallah that finger if you 'spect ta live, Jamaican-ass fool!"

A.J. tried, I'll give him that. He should have known he was a dead man. Hope is a motherfucker, though. He used his good hand to shove the finger down his throat, and he gagged on it. Big Dog had stepped behind him, moving Larry to the side. When A.J. leaned down to throw up, Big Dog came down with the axe—this time on his neck. The blow nearly severed his head. It probably would have if it weren't for the man's dreadlocks. The moment Big Dog finished the blow all hell broke open upon the scene.

The woods came alive! Five, six, seven sleek, dark-grey forms leapt from the shadows. They were snarling and ganged up over by the cabin. Wolves! I shot my pistol at the pack and heard a yelp as it hit one. My uncles started yelling. We all ran and jumped into the Lincoln as fast as we could. The shot must have scared the wolves enough to keep them back.

"What the muthah-fuck?" Larry yelled. I had ended up in

the driver's seat. The keys were in the ignition, so I cranked it, turned the lights revealing the scurrying, grey bodies, turned the car around, and hauled ass out of there. Big Dog was in the seat next to me. Once we had gotten a couple hundred feet down the dirt road, he started laughing.

"Man, take my ass back to Dallas," he said. Slim laughed with him and started talking.

I shook my head. Their laughter and Slim's annoying voice, along with my imagination's depiction of what the wolves were doing to poor A.J.'s body chased me back into feverish delirium.

There. That's it. I'm going to bed.

*The End of Part 1*

*Special Thanks to:*

*Adayiah*
*Sarah Bowen*
*Josh Davies*
*Kevin Klix*
*Madeline Reiss*
*Karla Silvas*
*Steve Spradlin*
*Steve Springer*
*Wanda Zamorano*
*Justin and Diane Fourton*
*Jason Robert Price*
*Mike Lyon*
*David Stevens*

Author *Jonathan Spradlin* currently resides in Old East Dallas. He spends as much time as he can with his daughter, his girlfriend, and his writing implements. He knows from hard-won experience that to do otherwise is to invite serious trouble.

CPSIA information can be obtained
at www.ICGtesting.com
Printed in the USA
FSOW01n0524051115
12987FS

9 780692 524787